Behold!
The Land
of Canaan

CHRONICLES OF THE HISTORY OF ITS
PEOPLE, PLACES AND PURSUITS

Written and Published by the
Tucker County Highlands History and Education Project
A Project of the Friends of the 500th

2011

Copy 1743 of 2000

International Standard Book Number 978-1-4507-6012-6
Copyright© 2011 by the Friends of the 500th
Tucker County Highlands History and Education Project
PO Box 422
Davis, West Virginia 26260

NOTICE TO USERS OF THIS BOOK

Behold! The Land of Canaan

Table of Contents

2-9   Elliott Ours: A Tribute to a Friend
by Dave Lesher for Behold! Volume 2

10-17   Riley Worden: In His Own Words
by Cindy Phillips, Chronicles 20, August 2008

18-21   Robert Eastham: A Transplanted Virginian
by Bruce Dalton, Chronicles 26, August 2009

22-27   Ab Crossland: Moonshiner Who Beat City Hall
by Chuck Nichols, Chronicles 31, June 2010

28-31   Bessie Harr Marries Canaan Valley Farmer
by Debra Lucille Harr, Chronicles 27, October 2009

32-61   Harr Family's 130 Years in Canaan Valley
by Dave Lesher for Behold! Volume 2

62-67   A Massive Mountain Weathered Away
by Dave Miller, Chronicles 36, April 2011

68-71   Childhood Memories of Canaan Heights
by Janice Hardman, Chronicles 22, December 2008

72-77   St. John's Lutheran Church in Davis
by Andy Dalton, Chronicles 29, February 2010

78-87   Mallow Family and Maple Grove Lake
by Dave Lesher, Chronicles 35, February 2011

88-93   Recalling "Twenty Feet from Glory"
by Elliott Ours, Chronicles 19, June 2008

94-103   Heitz Family and Legacy of Skiing
by Dave Lesher, Chronicles 30 & 32, April & August 2010

104-109   Hunting Heritage in the Highlands
by Cindy Phillips, Chronicles 33, October 2010

110-113   Canaan Valley's Historic Sites
by Andy Dalton, Chronicles 23, February 2009

114   About the Authors

115-122   Index

123   Map of the Tucker County Highlands and Vicinity

Preface

Two short years have flown by since our group of aspiring historians successfully published volume one of *Behold! The Land of Canaan* in June 2009. We were very grateful to receive a grant from the West Virginia Humanities Council that paid most of the cost to print 750 copies of that book, more than 200 of which were donated to schools, libraries, civic and charitable organizations, historical societies, and political leaders in Charleston and Washington, DC. Likewise, we were delighted to see how much interest *Behold!* generated and how quickly they moved in the Refuge Visitor Center bookstore for a small donation. We appreciate the support and encouragement received from the community during and since that time.

In the months that followed, as we reveled in our achievement, we continued to write and publish history articles that appeared in the Friends of the 500th bimonthly newsletter, *Timberdoodle*. Less than a year after *Behold!* appeared, we began planning to publish a second volume of new articles.

Regrettably, the joy and pride we felt in the summer of 2009 were heavily clouded by the passing of our friend Elliott Ours, who had been an important part of the ideas and energy behind the inception of our group, The Tucker County Highlands History and Education Project (TCHHEP), in 2004. We are pleased that the last Chronicles article Elliott wrote is included in this volume. But he is sadly missed by all of us.

Behold! The Land of Canaan volume two contains articles written by members of our board of editors plus four new contributors. Debra Harr and Janice Hardman wrote about their recollections of time spent in Canaan during the younger years of their lives, a refreshing read for those of us who enjoy knowing what it was like here in the not too distant "old days". Dave Miller and Chuck Nichols each picked topics they say always interested them; Dave focused on the interplay of the natural and cultural history of the Valley and Chuck explored the life of Ab Crossland, one of the Valley's legendary characters.

Although it is important to credit the authors of this edition of *Behold!*, it is equally notable to recognize those who worked the nuts and bolts of bringing this book into reality. As with the first volume, Julie Dzaack and Cindy Phillips served as copy editor/proofreader and graphic designer, respectively. Their technical and creative minds produced a professional final product. Remarkably, all of the time and effort for this publication was provided by volunteers.

Finally, a word of thanks to the Tucker Community Foundation for awarding the Friends of the 500th a $500 grant toward the purchase of the software and laptop computer to dedicate to this project. The remainder of the cash outlay was provided by TCHHEP fundraisers, donations and proceeds from volume one. As with volume one, all proceeds will further the mission of TCHHEP and future editions of *Behold! The Land of Canaan*.

All of us have had a memorable experience producing this new book of historic articles about the Tucker County highlands we love so much. We trust our readers will enjoy it.

> The mission of the Tucker County Highlands History and Education Project is to collect, document and preserve oral histories, augmented by other historical research as necessary, to chronicle the cultural and natural history of the Tucker County Highlands, making these accounts accessible to the public to encourage interest and education in our heritage.

Andy Dalton, Bruce Dalton, Julie Dzaack,
Dave Lesher and Cindy Phillips
The Tucker County Highlands History
and Education Project
Board of Editors
January 1, 2011

INSIDE—Chronicles of the History of the Tucker County Highlands

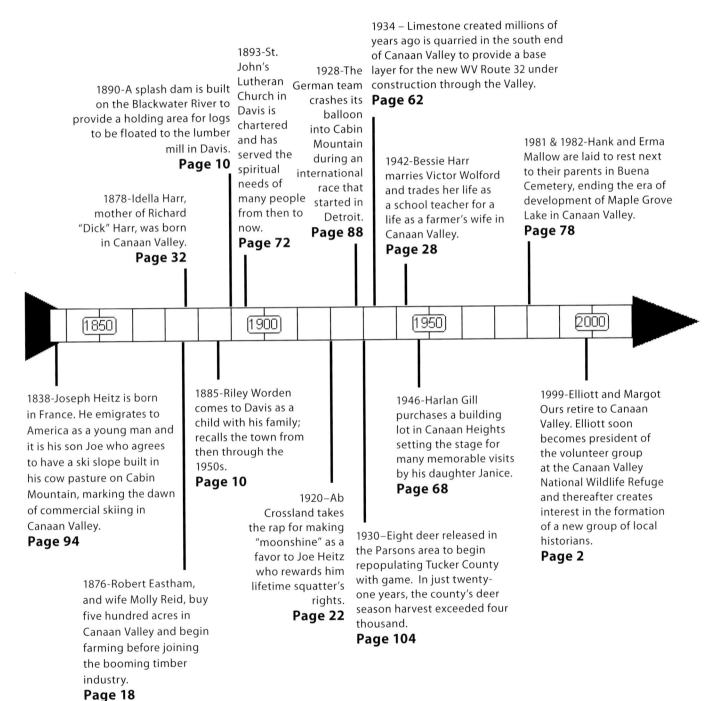

1934 – Limestone created millions of years ago is quarried in the south end of Canaan Valley to provide a base layer for the new WV Route 32 under construction through the Valley.
Page 62

1893-St. John's Lutheran Church in Davis is chartered and has served the spiritual needs of many people from then to now.
Page 72

1928-The German team crashes its balloon into Cabin Mountain during an international race that started in Detroit.
Page 88

1890-A splash dam is built on the Blackwater River to provide a holding area for logs to be floated to the lumber mill in Davis.
Page 10

1942-Bessie Harr marries Victor Wolford and trades her life as a school teacher for a life as a farmer's wife in Canaan Valley.
Page 28

1981 & 1982-Hank and Erma Mallow are laid to rest next to their parents in Buena Cemetery, ending the era of development of Maple Grove Lake in Canaan Valley.
Page 78

1878-Idella Harr, mother of Richard "Dick" Harr, was born in Canaan Valley.
Page 32

1838-Joseph Heitz is born in France. He emigrates to America as a young man and it is his son Joe who agrees to have a ski slope built in his cow pasture on Cabin Mountain, marking the dawn of commercial skiing in Canaan Valley.
Page 94

1885-Riley Worden comes to Davis as a child with his family; recalls the town from then through the 1950s.
Page 10

1946-Harlan Gill purchases a building lot in Canaan Heights setting the stage for many memorable visits by his daughter Janice.
Page 68

1999-Elliott and Margot Ours retire to Canaan Valley. Elliott soon becomes president of the volunteer group at the Canaan Valley National Wildlife Refuge and thereafter creates interest in the formation of a new group of local historians.
Page 2

1920–Ab Crossland takes the rap for making "moonshine" as a favor to Joe Heitz who rewards him lifetime squatter's rights.
Page 22

1930–Eight deer released in the Parsons area to begin repopulating Tucker County with game. In just twenty-one years, the county's deer season harvest exceeded four thousand.
Page 104

1876-Robert Eastham, and wife Molly Reid, buy five hundred acres in Canaan Valley and begin farming before joining the booming timber industry.
Page 18

A Tribute
To a Friend

Behold! The Land of Canaan Volume Two is dedicated to our very good friend and mentor, Elliott Ours. It was in 2004 that his idea of collecting oral histories from senior citizens in the Canaan Valley area got us started writing vignettes of history to be published in *Timberdoodle*, the bimonthly newsletter of the Friends of the 500th (the Friends). By 2009, eighteen of those stories were published in volume one of *Behold! The Land of Canaan.* We were driven by the inspiration Elliott brought to our little group of aspiring historians. Sadly, just a month after the book was printed, Elliott passed away. But he had a chance to see the book, and we knew he shared the pride we all felt for what had been accomplished. We are honored that Elliott's last article (See "Recalling the Story of Twenty Feet from Glory", page 88) is included in this volume and that one of his many photographs taken from his home atop Cabin Mountain graces the cover. As a tribute to his life, work and inspiration, we present a vignette about the man we knew and respected so much.

Willis Elliott Ours was born in Clarksburg on December 2, 1934, the only child of Willis and Marguerite Fleming Ours. Preferring his middle name, he was always *Elliott* to family and friends. With family roots deep in the Allegheny highlands, Elliott's great grandfather, Frank J. Bell, was a coal miner in Elk Garden before 1900; in 1905 he was the mine foreman at the hamlet of Beacon, located along Beaver Creek, about five miles upstream from Davis.

Ten-year old Elliott poses with, L to R, his mother Marguerite Fleming Ours, grandmother Sadie Bell Ours, and great-grandmother Elizabeth Bell. Photo taken at the home of Sadie Bell Ours on Euclid Avenue in Thomas, WV, and courtesy of Margot Ours.

Frank and Elizabeth Bell had a daughter Sadie (among other children) who grew up and married Bernie Edward Ours; they had three children, Robert, John and Willis. Willis married Marguerite Fleming, who was born in the little town of Schell, West Virginia and later relocated to Thomas, West Virginia. Their son Elliott is whom we are celebrating in this story.

As a youngster, Elliott attended elementary school in Thomas. When he was ten years old, his parents divorced, and he and his mother went to Clarksburg to stay with her family. Returning to Thomas a few years later, Elliott lived with his grandparents Edward and Sadie Ours while his mother attended beauty school in Martinsburg. Afterward, she returned to Thomas and opened a beauty shop on Front Street.

Elliott graduated from Thomas High School in 1952 and began attending West Virginia University that fall. However his heart was not in it, and he did not return to Morgantown for a second year. In September 1953, Elliott signed on for a three-year hitch in the US Army.

Life in the Army seemed to ignite Elliott's interests. Following basic training, he attended communications school and from there shipped out to West Germany. He was assigned to a radio listening post near the border with East Germany where the Army was conducting secret operations of intercepting Soviet communications.

In the closing months of Elliott's time in Germany, an unexpected development occurred that would influence his life anew; he met the lovely, young Fräulein Margot Benthien. Soon thereafter, Elliott introduced his friend George Wilson to Margot's sister Renate. From then on, the two sisters were in the company of Elliott and George as often as possible for the remainder of the boys' time in Germany. Elliott returned to the US in September 1956 and was discharged from the Army. George stayed in Germany until he and Renate were married, then he returned to the US where he was discharged. It was not until late March 1957 that Margot and Renate were able to travel to the US. Elliott and George were waiting at the pier in New York City when they

arrived. Elliott Ours and Margot Benthien were married in Clarksburg on April 14, 1957. The foursome would remain close for the many years that followed.

Newlyweds Elliott and Margot set up housekeeping in an apartment next door to where Elliott's mother, Marguerite, was living. A few months later she married Charlie Topper, a childhood sweetheart from her school days in Thomas.

In the fall of 1957, Elliott and Margot moved to Morgantown where he returned to West Virginia University as a full time student. Margot's English had improved enough that she was able to get a job in the university bookstore. Her wages, along with Elliott's GI Bill benefits, enabled them to rent on-campus housing for $30 a month and otherwise make ends meet. No car, of course.

Elliott (center)
posing with two Army buddies in
the early 1950s. Photo courtesy of Margot Ours.

Elliott graduated in June 1961 with a BS in electrical engineering. He found a job with the Federal Communications Commission (FCC) and was assigned to their office in Detroit, Michigan. With their new prosperity and the promise of more to come, Elliott and Margot's first child, Michele, was born in 1964, followed by Tom in 1968.

Shortly after Tom was born, Elliott was promoted to a position with the FCC in Washington, DC. They first rented a townhouse in Wheaton, Maryland, and then in February 1969, bought a house near Suitland, Maryland. This was their home for the next nine years.

In 1978, with Michele approaching high school age, Elliott was determined to move his family away from what he saw as the ever-worsening influences on teenage life in the local community where they lived. They purchased a ten acre tract of land near Shepherdstown, West Virginia, had a new home built and moved in 1979. Here Michele and Tom went to school in the fresh air and wide open spaces of the West Virginia panhandle. Elliott busied himself caring for their new home and yard while a local farmer cut hay from the remainder of the acreage. He rode the daily train into Washington, DC and transferred to the Metro to ride to his office. It was a long commute, but he enjoyed the quiet time to think or read or just take a nap.

Elliott and Margot pose in front of the beautiful scenery of Lake Louise, Alberta during a visit in August 2001. Photo courtesy of Margot Ours.

In 1989 Elliott reached the requisite age of fifty-five with thirty years of federal service (which included his time in the Army) to retire with full benefits. On December 31, he and Margot entered into that new phase of their lives. Michele and Tom were grown –Tom would soon finish college and both were off into lives of their own. Margot became involved with the local orchestra, and both of them gave time to the Lutheran Church where they were members.

Retirement gave Elliott some time to attend to his interest in both his and Margot's ancestral roots in Germany. Over the years he had been slowly assembling a genealogy of the Ours family from which he was descended. Now with the freedom of retirement, he and Margot traveled to Germany to research their family trees and revisit the place where they had met nearly forty years earlier. The trip was successful beyond his hopes–they found the church where records showed the names and date of the marriage of the couple that subsequently emigrated to America in the 1750s and from which Elliott was directly descended. Their last name was *Auer*, and it was easy to understand how its pronunciation would eventually change the spelling to *Ours*. Elliott savored the victory of learning the identity of his g-g-g-g-g-grandparents.

As Elliott's years as a retiree passed by, he grew weary of the work to maintain their large home and tract of land. More and more people were moving to the Shepherdstown area and along with that came the noise and traffic and distractions of suburban sprawl. Elliott and Margot became grandparents in 1996, and Elliott wondered about moving to a less congested environment for the benefit of his grandchildren, just as he and Margot had done twenty years earlier for their children. More and more, Elliott's thoughts turned to moving back to Tucker County. Despite Margot having some uncertainty about making such a change at that point in their lives, they sold their home in 1999 and relocated to Canaan Valley. They bought a home in the Timberline community, located near the summit of Cabin Mountain and commanding a magnificent, sweeping view of the Valley. Surrounded by the beauty of this place in all four seasons, Elliott pursued his

Behold! The Land of Canaan

passion for nature photography with a new fervor. The Canaan Valley National Wildlife Refuge soon caught his interest, and he began working as a volunteer and joining in meetings of the volunteer group the Friends. Elliott's interest and enthusiasm as a volunteer vaulted him into the position of president of the Friends in November 2001.

Margot sits with George and Renate Wilson on Easter 2010. Elliott introduced George to Margot's sister Renate when he and George were stationed in Germany in the 1950s. George and Renate live in Tennessee.

One of Elliott's early tasks as president was to begin construction of the Freeland Trail, an accessible boardwalk from Freeland Road to a beaver pond overlook. With funding provided through a National Fish and Wildlife Foundation grant and labor provided by volunteers, the task began as the last of winter's snowdrifts were melting in the spring of 2003 and was completed as the first snow flurries began that fall. The large group of volunteers that turned out in the opening days of the work quickly dwindled to a handful of regulars as the work wore on through that summer. But it was Elliott who pressed his team of volunteers to return to the work each week, keeping their hands on the task and their minds on the goal. Funding from the grant was also used to build information kiosks and procure interpretive panels for the Freeland Trail boardwalk, the Old Timberline Road parking area and at White Grass Ski Touring Center. In addition to the new boardwalk built during Elliott's time as president, the Friends built a footbridge over Sand Run on the Middle Ridge Trail and the swinging bridge at Camp 70 was redecked.

Elliott always made education, particularly youth education, one of his priorities. In his first "From the President" column in *Timberdoodle*, he highlighted education as one of his primary goals. With that guiding philosophy, the Friends developed a close partnership with another Tucker County youth education initiative, Tucker County Connections (TCC). TCC had already been conducting an annual three-day educational outing called Fifth Grade Connections for Tucker County fifth-graders,

"Imagine the satisfaction of being part of a program which helps to produce a new generation of young people who better appreciate the natural world and our Refuge."

Elliott's enthusiasm for youth education shone through in this statement from his "From the President" column in the June 2006 issue of *Timberdoodle*.

Elliott Ours
A Life's Legacy in Photos

With grandchildren Andrew and Anna Kate, 2009. Photo courtesy of Margot Ours.

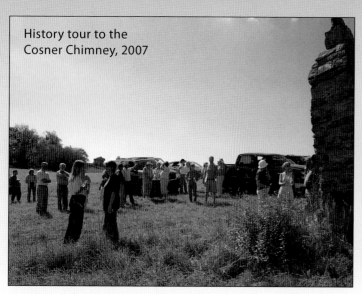

History tour to the
Cosner Chimney, 2007

Working on the Freeland Trail
boardwalk, 2003

Leading the Friends annual membership meeting, 2006

Elliott speaking to attendees at the dedication of a time capsule at the Refuge Visitor Center in 2003, marking the centennial of the founding of the first National Wildlife Refuge.

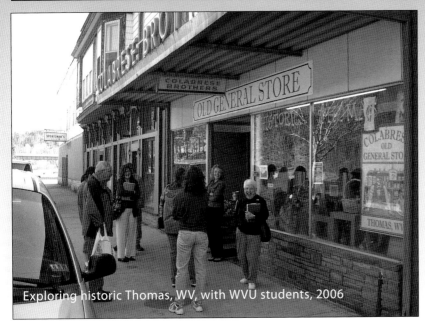

Exploring historic Thomas, WV, with WVU students, 2006

Hats off to a virgin red spruce found in Canaan Valley, 2007

Chronicles of Its History

and Elliott encouraged the Friends to donate (*Tribute* continued on page 8)funds to help TCC meet its resource needs and create scholarships for families needing financial assistance to attend. The Friends also provided volunteers for part of the three-day event. Augmenting what the Friends had donated to TCC, the Friends began a program of funding the cost of school bus transportation to bring elementary and middle school classes to the Refuge Visitor Center each fall for a full day of educational sessions aimed at teaching wildlife conservation, the basics of biology and an overall appreciation of the outdoors. This very successful program came to be called Wild School, and it continues today as an annual event each September.

Through his love of photography, Elliott proposed a project called "Learning about Nature through Photography". Another National Fish and Wildlife Foundation grant was successfully written, and in the summer of 2006, several groups of school-age children spent two days on the Refuge with SLR digital cameras taking photos and learning about flora and fauna on the Refuge. Led by Elliott and other local adult volunteers, photos were then reviewed and discussed at the Refuge Visitor Center. A few weeks later a show of their work, now printed and matted, was attended by friends and families of the young photographers.

Among Elliott's most notable legacies during his time as the Friends' president was his idea to collect oral histories from some of the senior residents of Canaan Valley. He proposed that these oral histories would serve as a source of information from which to prepare local history feature articles to appear in *Timberdoodle*. What started as a notion to increase interest in the Friends' newsletter blossomed into an active committee of the Friends conducting oral histories, taking history walks, conducting an inventory of historic sites in Canaan Valley and writing– about all this and more. The history committee formally adopted the name Tucker County Highlands History and Education Project (TCHHEP) in the summer of 2004 and has been actively meeting and working since then. In 2009, the first eighteen history articles that appeared in *Timberdoodle* under the banner *Chronicles of TCHHEP* were compiled and published in a 128-page book entitled *Behold! The Land of Canaan*. In the meantime, *Chronicles* feature articles continued to appear in each *Timberdoodle* and this volume two of *Behold! The Land of Canaan* is a collection of all new *Chronicles*.

Another of Elliott's initiatives was lobbying the West Virginia Division of Highways to install signs in Davis and Canaan Valley directing visitors to Refuge trailhead access points. The development of trails on the Refuge was another of his priorities, and he provided a number of ideas to raise the public awareness of trail use by hikers, bikers, skiers and horseback riders aimed at developing a greater appreciation of the Valley's beauty and history. Coincident with Elliott's focus on Refuge trails was the start-up of the Adopt-a-Trail project by the Friends whereby volunteers would periodically hike each trail, reporting on its condition and need for repair.

After five notable years of service to the Friends, Elliott stepped down as president in October 2006. In the years that followed, he continued to be actively involved as a Friends member, contributor to *Chronicles* and as an advisor and counselor to new officers and members of the board of directors.

One of Elliott's visions was that of making the Refuge Visitor Center a focus for youth education in Canaan Valley. For him, it held great potential for becoming a place with a nature center and auditorium for programs held year-round both indoors and out. In early 2009, he developed a concept and plan of construction incorporating these ideas for the Refuge Visitor Center and presented it to the Refuge staff and Friends board of directors. The far-reaching concept of Elliott's ideas was impressive in scope and the Refuge staff promised to include it in the long-term planning that was underway.

Unfortunately, time was not on Elliott's side. His health slowly declined as spring turned to summer, and he quietly passed away at the home of his daughter, Michele, on July 14, 2009. In the midst of our feelings of loss we were grateful for the contributions he left behind as reminders of his service. Here we commemorate our friend and mentor Elliott Ours.

People

Stories

In His Own Words: Riley Worden Talks of the Early Years in Davis

The following information was excerpted from a written transcript of an oral interview conducted in 1958 with Davis resident, Riley Worden. The interview, conducted by Dr. O.D. Lambert and Charles Shetler of West Virginia University, is housed at West Virginia University and is made available courtesy of the West Virginia and Regional History Collection. Mr. Worden arrived in Davis as a child in 1885 and witnessed first-hand the many changes the town experienced over the next eight decades. His priceless account serves as a reminder of the growth and activity associated with the logging industry in the highlands of Tucker County. Readers should be aware that Mr. Worden's account of events and his timelines associated with them may not always appear to agree with those of others; a fact that only points out the challenges faced by today's historians in reconstructing a truly factual narrative of our past.

Dr. Lambert: This is June 17, 1958. We are in the Worden's Hotel in Davis, West Virginia. Mr. Charles Shetler, Curator of the Archives of West Virginia University and Mr. Riley Worden of Davis, West Virginia are present. This is O.D. Lambert who is speaking. We have come to Davis for the purpose of making a recording of Mr. Worden. Mr. Worden, will you tell us where you were born?

Mr. Worden: I was born in Hampshire County, Moorefield Junction. That is 6 miles from Romney.

Lambert: ...and the date?

Worden: 1882, the 14th day of May.

Lambert: When did you come to Davis, Mr. Worden?

Worden: We came here, my father moved here it was about the middle of 1885 and we moved into the Blackwater Hotel, but it wasn't finished and my father opened up the Blackwater Hotel for the

Behold! The Land of Canaan

Davis's. [Henry Gassaway, Thomas, and William Davis]

Lambert: Tell us about the condition of the town of Davis when you came here in 1885.

Worden: When we came here there were only just a few houses, about 16 and 18 houses here then, maybe 20 houses. There were a couple of boarding houses near a place called the West Virginia House. That's out by the tannery. That's when they were building the tannery.

Lambert: When were the mills built in Davis?

Worden: Rumbarger, he started his mill in 1885.

Lambert: Where was it located?

Worden: Right down here across from the depot, where the mill always stood. Right below this big bridge down here, you can see a lot of the concrete stuff down there.

Lambert: ...and the Rumbargers sold their plant to the Thompsons?

Worden: They sold out to the Blackwater Boom and Lumber Company. Mr. Thompson came in here, he bought a lot of timber up in the swampy land here and he was going to float it down the river too. Rumbarger then went to Elkins and put in a mill up around Mill Creek. When Mr. Thompson came in he built a mill down below town here a mile, before Babcock put in a hardwood mill. But he just had the framework up and that is what started Blackwater Boom and Lumber Company. Then they sold that mill to Beaver Creek Lumber Company up

here. The man who put it in was Jag Allen from Hagerstown and they took all the timber out back on the land.

Lambert: How many mills were built in Davis?

Worden: Well, the Blackwater Mill burned down twice and they rebuilt it, and the Beaver Creek never did burn down. That ran until they had all the timber, mostly all, cut out and they only took the best timber. There was so much timber cut in those days out in this section, at Pendleton Run, out there. A man named Burger had a mill down at Pendleton Run that is 2 ½ miles from here, and he had a big mill down at Douglas. They only took the best timber. The hemlock lumber sawed only brought $6 a thousand [board feet] and the best of spruce only brought $18 a thousand. Mr. Burger cut this big timber down anywhere from 4 to 5 foot across the tree and just took the bark and left the timber lay and rot, and they did that all over this country.

Lambert: Mr. Worden, tell us about the operation of the mill and the cutting of timber and the floating of the timber down the Blackwater.

Worden: They had no log trains in here in the beginning and most of the logs was floated down the river. Mr. A. [Albert] Thompson and his son Frank floated the logs down to their sawmill. They had three splash dams. [A *splash dam* is a temporary wooden structure used to raise the water level in streams to float logs downstream to sawmills.] They had one on Sand Run and one on Little Blackwater [River] and the big one up here 2 ½ miles above Davis. All the logs came into that dam and then they would open

An 1885 photo of the town of Davis, then little more than a clearing in the forest filled with tree stumps and a few of the first of the town's buildings. This is the same year that three-year-old Riley Worden arrived here with his family. This photo, courtesy of Ruth Cooper Allman, has appeared in many publications, but it is unknown to whom it should be credited.

Davis in 1885. This map of Davis was created by T.M. (Thaddeus Mortimer) Fowler who, in the late 19th century and early 20th century, produced maps that captured snapshots in time of burgeoning communities in the eastern United States. Source, Library of Congress, Maps Collections, for more examples of Fowler Maps go to the Library of Congress Panoramic Maps Collection at http://memory.loc.gov/ammem/pmhtml/panhome.html.

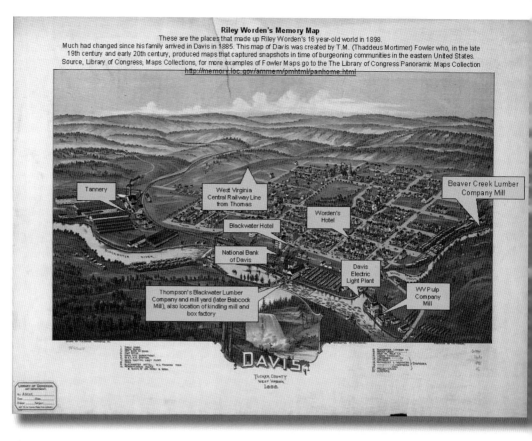

Riley Worden's Memory Map

These are the places that made up Riley Worden's 16 year-old world in 1898. Much had changed since his family arrived in Davis in 1885. This map of Davis was created by T.M. (Thaddeus Mortimer) Fowler who, in the late 19th century and early 20th century, produced maps that captured snapshots in time of burgeoning communities in the eastern United States. Source, Library of Congress, Maps Collections, for more examples of Fowler Maps go to the The Library of Congress Panoramic Maps Collection http://memory.loc.gov/ammem/pmhtml/panhome.html

the booms for about an hour and let the water bring the logs on down to the mill out here in Davis. While Rumbargers were in here they only took out the timber, the cherry lumber. They hauled that in from Canaan Valley in big sleds. They didn't float that, they hauled that.

Lambert: That was done during the winter season?

Worden: Yes, during the winter season.

Lambert: Tell us a little more about the Rumbarger operations cutting the cherry and walnut and bringing it in on bobsleds.

Worden: They did that for a couple of years. The snow in those days came along in October and it stayed until April. It never left then the way it does now. It might have been because of the big timber being here, what kept the winters cold. You know back years ago up at your home the winters were colder and lasted longer.

Lambert: What conveyance would they use to bring the sleds in? Would they have horses?

Worden: They used horses. When Mr. Thompson came in here he brought some oxen in with him from up in Ridgway [Pennsylvania]. They used the oxen where they couldn't use horses, in the swamps, and skidded the logs out with them. [*Skidding* is a method of transporting logs by pulling them from a location by horse, oxen, or mechanical systems.] I forget just what year it was they came in.

Lambert: Tell us about Mr. Babcock buying the Thompson's out, Mr. Worden.

Worden: Mr. Babcock came in from Pittsburgh. Him and his two brothers came in and they were here just a few days buying Mr. Thompson out. When they bought Mr. Thompson out they put in a lot of improvement on the mill and then they brought the trees in, all of the whole tree, and tried it. It would take two of the long flat cars to

Behold! The Land of Canaan

haul the trees in and they had a jig saw across from the mill where they sawed this up into logs instead of hauling the log in. They ran that for a couple of years but that wasn't a success, so they went back to cutting the logs anywhere from fourteen feet up to twenty feet. Mr. Babcock had brought in the skidders which Mr. Thompson had never used. They took the timber out of the [Blackwater] Canyon with these skidders where Mr. Thompson was going to build a mill down there in a place called Lime Rock. He was going to cut his timber in the Canyon and float it down [to] Lime Rock to his mill down there. [*Lime Rock* was a small mill community on the Blackwater River, a short distance upstream of the town of Hendricks, WV.] Of course, all the timber in high grounds he brought that in on log trains or he couldn't have gotten it out of the Canyon by trains. Mr. Babcock had put in a lot of switchbacks down the Canyon and took quite a bit out, what he didn't get out with skidders. Then he took most of the timber out on both sides of the Canyon on the right hand side of the Western Maryland Railroad, what went down to Hendricks. He took that all out on skidders across the railroad over on the other mountain

and that is where they dropped them. Then they loaded them up with loaders and loaded the log trains.

Lambert: About how many camps did they have in Canaan Valley when they were operating in the Valley?

Worden: Mr. Thompson had about five lumber camps and then Mr. Babcock, after he got up in there, he took out so much timber out of the sawmill with skidders, he had in there three or four camps up there. Then they kept on building the railroad. They bought a lot of timber over in Grant County. They bought enough timber to run twenty years over there. Mr. Viering was a woods superintendent for Mr. Babcock, and he was coming in from Stony River Dam one evening. It was raining and the old gentleman had a straight-connected engine and when he got at the top of the hill he didn't put the brakes on quick enough so the engine got away from him. He had five cars on, flat cars. The men on the train was a fireman, a conductor, and another man. They jumped off the train and Mr. Viering came down into the lowlands at a pretty bad curve and the engine turned over and killed him. It buried him in the mud. Well, after that Mr. Babcock then sold all his timber out over in Grant County to people that had small portable sawmills. He quit business then, so that finished up our lumber business. If Mr. Viering could have only lived, our sawmill could have run twenty years longer than what it did.

Lambert: Could you tell us about how much lumber one of the mills sawed a day?

Worden: They would run anywhere from 100 to 150 thousand [board feet] a day. [One *board foot* is equal to 12" x 12" x 1".] Now Mr. Thompson, he made a cut down hill one time – it was all big timber – ship timber, it was 248 thousand he cut that day, but it was all big timber, square timber such as 10 x 10, 10 x 12, and stuff like that. That was the biggest cut ever made in his mill but

Photo of work horses standing by the barn on the cattle and horse farm run by the Babcock Lumber Company located on Beaver Creek several miles upstream from Davis. Notice the size of the horses compared to the boy tending them. Photo courtesy of Ruth Cooper Allman who says it was given to her by Bretzel Lang, son of B. O. Lang (1884-1969) who was born on the farm.

after Babcock got here he put in 3 saws – band saws, in his mill where Mr. Thompson had a circular saw and one band saw. They got so then that was only teeth on one side of the saw. They put in them double cut saws with the teeth on both sides of the saw. That sawed it going and coming back too.

Lambert: Mr. Worden, you haven't told us about the box factory and kindling mill. Could you tell us something about that?

Worden: Well, Mr. Thompson put the box factory in here. They made flooring, siding, and boxes – just the ends, the sides and the tops – you see. They were nailed together with strips on top and they were all run through a machine to put that edge on like flooring has – you know that groove and that tongue groove. Then they had these big slabs of two inch iron where they nailed these on to clinch the nails. That ran for years and that is where they planed all the lumber. They had a planing mill in there too, where they planed the spruce and the good lumber. When Babcock came in he took out a lot of hardwood down over in Grant County. Well, he made an awful lot of flooring. Mr. Thompson never cut any hardwoods; he only cut the spruce

or hemlock.

Shetler: Did they make shingles there?

Worden: We did on Beaver Creek. They had a shingle wood [factory] making shingles up there. They had it in there for about three years. They made shingles out of the hemlock. A lot of the ends on big trees would be kind of hollow and they would saw them off and haul them in on the log train to the kindling wood mill. They had a thing there that sawed these blocks off the length that the shingles were to be, and they had a machine there to square them off and they would keep running it back and forth in this machine to make the shingles. Then they had the ones that piled, they laid these shingles into the piles so many shingles was in a bundle.

Lambert: Did they have a kindling factory?

Worden: Yes, the kindling wood factory came in just about ten years before Babcock shut the plant down. They came in from up in Pennsylvania and New York state and put this kindling wood mill in. They worked about fifty or sixty men and girls. They had a wooden box about 2 ½ inches long and then they had these pressers, and from this big drive they had a big building about eighty foot high with nothing but

The first sawmill in Davis was established in 1886, when the J.L. Rumbarger Lumber Company began sawing hardwoods. A succession of companies followed. The Babcock Lumber and Boom Company (pictured here in 1911) began operating in Davis in 1907. Its predecessor was the Thompson Lumber Company. The Babcock mill operated until 1924, bringing to a close nearly forty years of continuously operating mill operations in Davis. Photo courtesy of USDA Forest Service.

Behold! The Land of Canaan

steam pipes. Then in another place where these slabs would come from they would saw these all up into little blocks and they would go into this elevator and take them up into the top of this high building where all of these steam pipes were. There were three miles of steam pipes in there – 2 inch pipes or 2 ½ inch pipes – I guess they were. They dried these and they came down these shoots to where each man had his press. Then they would work putting these blocks in about the shape of an egg—they were about nine inches through and about ten inch high—shaped like an egg. They would then put them in this press, set their foot on the lever, and it was an air machine that pressed them all tight together. They tied string around each of these bundles of kindling and they were shipped to the cities to start their fires within the city. I think they got two cents a bunch for those bundles, and some of those girls made anywhere from $12 to $14 a day for bundling kindling wood. It was pretty fast. Then a lot of men came down from up in New York state – professional kindling wood bundlers. It was might nice in there. It was a good and warm in there and they had high stools to sit on and it was might nice work for some, and we had lots of women here in Davis that bundled wood. We have a woman cooking down there – she worked down at the kindling wood mill for five years.

Shetler: How did the timber operator acquire land for cutting [timber] or acquire the wood?

Worden: Well, often time Mr. Thompson and different people who ran the mills here contracted by the thousand to cut the timber for them, so much a thousand they got for cutting the timber and putting it through the skidway. Beaver Creek [Lumber Company] hauled all of their logs on log cars but they had to load them by hand. They rolled them up those spike skids until they got the car loaded. But in later years they used loaders and they didn't have to have people load them by hand. That was hard work rolling those big logs up on those cars.

Lambert: About how many men were occupied in Davis when all the mills were in operation?

Worden: There must have been around twelve or fouteen hundred. Of course, that is not including the men who worked in the woods because Babcock had twelve hundred men working in

The West Virginia Pulp and Paper Company (pictured here in 1911) in Davis was built in 1895 by the Luke brothers. The extensive building complex stood on the east bank of Beaver Creek, near the confluence with the Blackwater River. At one time the plant employed four hundred workers. In 1919, workers went on strike in sympathy for fellow workers in Tyrone, Pennsylvania. Response from the mill owners was to close the mill and never reopen. Operations were moved, but remnants of the buildings slowly deteriorated over many decades. Eventually most physical evidence of operations disappeared. Photo courtesy of USDA Forest Service.

the woods when he had all of his camps in here. He brought in a bunch of Austrians from up in Ashtola [Pennsylvania] in here and he used mostly Austrians. Of course, they had their own camps and the Americans, they had their own camps where they stayed at.

Lambert: Where did the woodsmen come from when they came into Davis?

Worden: They came from around Pennsylvania, Ridgway. Babcock's, they came from Ashtola and Johnstown [Pennsylvania]. He had another big mill at Winfred, Pennsylvania, and when he cut out, he brought them all in here. We had so many woodsmen come in from up New York state and Michigan. They came in from every place. We had a lot come in from Tennessee in here.

Lambert: Will you tell us about the woodsmen?

Worden: The woodmen were a good class of people. They were a good class of people, but they drank. They worked hard. They would go back and work two or three months in the woods and they would have a couple hundred dollars, but that wouldn't last them two days. Everybody that went in the saloon had to drink. Well they didn't go back to work for two or three weeks, but they never went hungry. Most of them, when they were broke, would go down to the sawmill and sleep in the sawdust or in the shavings when they had no money. But they were a good class of people. They were people that never did any killing, but they did a lot of fighting when they got drunk, and they would have some pretty big fights at the bars. I heard two men who thought they were the best. They would go out on the other side of the pulp mill, out of the corporation [town limits], and fight it out. When they knew there was a big fight going to be on, everyone would go over there. There would be anywhere from fifty to seventy-five people to go over and see who the best man was. They would fight that out and then they would get up and shake hands

Canaan Valley woodsmen pose for a photo during their break for lunch, ca.1905. Fred Cooper, father of Virginia Cooper Parsons, is seated in back, fourth from left. Frank Cooper, father of Ruth Cooper Allman, is at far left. Photo courtesy of Virginia Cooper Parsons.

with each other and then they would come back and go to drinking again. That is the kind of people they were.

Shetler: What time did they start work in the lumber camps?

Worden: They started at six o'clock in the morning in the summertime. They'd work eleven hours in the summertime. Of course, in the fall of the year, when the days got short, they didn't work that long. There was a lot of people that just traveled these camps around that didn't want work, but you never asked for a job in a lumber camp. You would go in the lobby [a room

in the logging camp building for socializing] and sit there in the morning. If the boss didn't ask you to go to work, you knew you didn't have any job, but you never asked for a job. They would stay there two or three days, and then they would go to another camp.

Shetler: What did they eat for breakfast?

Worden: These lumber camps were the finest places in the world to eat. Thompson, he fed fine. They had the finest cook they could get. Mr. Babcock, his cooks were the finest. They had to have the best of everything. If they didn't have the best, the workers went to some other camp. They had everything that you would get in a good hotel. They had the finest kind of meat. They would have steak, pork chops, bacon and eggs and everything. They had these long tables that had nothing but grub on them. They never kept anything that was left over. That went into the slop bucket for the hogs. They had to have the best for the woodsmen, and if the cooks weren't good, the woodsmen would quit and go to another camp.

Lambert: How did they deliver the food to the camps?

Worden: They hauled that in on the log trains, on the caboose. Their meat...they had ice boxes where they hauled meat up to the camp there. They didn't have electric refrigerators in those days.

Lambert: Did they have slaughterhouses here at Davis where they prepared their meat for their lumbermen?

Worden: Babcock did, Babcock had about twelve hundred head of cattle on his ranch up here. Babcock went to work and he fenced in sixteen or eighteen thousand acres. He put in all locust posts and five wire strands of barb wire around his property. Then he put in twelve hundred head of the finest heifer cattle there was and had the finest bulls to take care of them. Fellow named John Burley and a man named Kramer ran a meat shop for him in Davis. He had a man that did the butchering. He would butcher anywhere from eighteen to twenty-five cattle a week for the camps. So then they went to work and – Babcock he was pretty slick – he fenced all this land and he cleaned a lot of land up in here about four to five miles up above Davis... made fields out of it. He knew that the West

Behold! The Land of Canaan

Penn Power Company was going to come in here and build a big dam. So by having this land fenced in and everything, he sold out to the West Penn Power Company and got $600,000 for the land after the timber and everything was taken off. The West Penn bought a few farms and a lot of property here in town where the water [behind the dam] would have come up to it. They paid $117 an acre for a lot of land up there in Canaan. I wouldn't give $10 an acre for. They had to get the land because the water would come in. So the West Penn changed this road over here [Route 32] and put it around the mountain in Canaan away from the water. The other way going to Canaan Valley there at Cortland, they would have had three mile or more to put up a concrete bridge twelve feet high of the water. So it was cheaper for the West Penn Power Company to put this road around the mountain than it was to build that bridge. They put this bridge in over here and then they bought our electric light plant out here at Davis. Then they built us three dams here at Davis and these dams furnished the water for the reservoir over here. Of course, they had to pump that water in, but when the pulp mill was running we got our water for $80 a month [for the whole town]. The paper mill, or the pulp mill, pumped it to the town. Well that was very cheap, so we had everything nice when the pulp mill was here.

Shetler: When did the Power Company come into Davis, Mr. Worden?

Worden: The West Penn bought our electric plant out here in Davis about twenty-five or twenty-six years ago [1932 or 1933]. Mr. Thompson, he had a lot of timber left when he sold to Babcock. Then Babcock sold all of his land to the West Penn Power Company. He got $600,000 for it and he took $100,000 in money and $500,000 in stock in the West Penn Power Company. Well, the West Penn got permission from the legislature and from the Public Service to build these two big dams. They got the injunction out and it came before the Supreme Court of West Virginia and the Supreme Court turned it down – didn't let them build it. They were up here about three miles above Davis where they were going to build the dam – the big dam. That would have covered fifty-two miles around – pretty near all of Canaan Valley. They paid the Davis Coal and Coke Company off for the amount of coal what the water would cover on their coal land, so they bought them off and they withdrew their injunction. They were going to build one right above the Blackwater Falls and were going to tunnel over on the other stream that come down from Thomas. That is where they were going to have their big electric plant. Well, I am glad they didn't build because that would have spoiled a lot of my hunting. Of course, I can't hunt any more now.

Lambert: You have made an excellent recording Mr. Worden, and we thank you very much for our time and trouble that you have spent with us.

Worden: Oh, you are certainly welcome for it.

This sketch shows a proposed lake nearly nine miles in length, southwest to northeast, and as much as two miles in width in some places. Despite its size, if the dam had been built and the lake filled, it is interesting to note that not a single occupied dwelling or building in Canaan Valley would have been affected. That is because for years, local citizens were convinced the future lake was a certainty and made sure that all new construction was located above 3190' mean sea level, the planned lake water level (see "The Plan to Flood Canaan Valley", *Chronicles No. 17*, in *Behold! The Land of Canaan 2009* for more information about the long history of this project and the eventual outcome that led to the creation of the Canaan Valley National Wildlife Refuge).

Robert W. Eastham was born on February 28, 1842, and grew up in Rappahannock County, Virginia. He was the first born of eleven children to Benjamin Franklin and Lucy Eliza Browning Eastham.

Almost immediately after Virginia's secession from the Union, Eastham joined the Confederate Army. During the summer of 1863 he served with Colonel William E. Jones and Brigadier General Imboden in the capture of Rowlesburg, Kingwood and Morgantown, West Virginia. It is likely that on these raids Eastham first saw the unsettled area of Canaan Valley. During the Civil War, Eastham also served with Mosby's Rangers, a group of cavalry irregulars that staged raids against Union troops occupying northern Virginia. Among his fellow soldiers he earned the nickname "Bob Ridley" for his fiddle playing antics.

The Move to Canaan Valley

After the Civil War, Eastham returned home and began farming. In 1869 he married Mary "Molly" Reid, daughter of a local physician. In 1876, for reasons unknown, the Easthams moved to Tucker County, West Virginia. They purchased five hundred acres from Molly's father Dr. A.W. Reid and began farming in Canaan Valley. The area was mostly wilderness for many miles. The only others in the Valley at that time were the families of Solomon Cosner, John Nine and James Freeland.

Robert Eastham quickly became a well known and respected figure in the area and, in 1882, ran for a state legislative seat from Tucker and Randolph counties. Although Eastham lost the election, he continued to have an influence in local politics and led a drive to establish two new districts in Tucker County, the Fairfax and Davis districts. Following

an overwhelming vote in April 1893 to move the location of the Tucker County seat, Eastham was recruited to be one of the leaders who raided the St. George Court House and moved its contents to the new location in Parsons in August of that year. Despite calls for punishment, none of the bandits were ever charged with a crime.

Entering the Booming Timber Industry

Eastham continued to farm until 1883 when he was approached by Jacob Rumbarger, a lumberman searching the Valley for stands of cherry. This marked the start of Eastham's involvement in business ventures involving the area's timber resources. Continuing with these business interests, Eastham signed a contract with Henry Gassaway Davis, US Senator and President of the West Virginia and Pittsburg Railway, to organize and supervise the building of what would become the town of Davis. Work began in March 1884; by 1895 the town had grown to a population of three thousand, with six hundred dwellings. In 1886 Eastham returned his focus to lumbering and began cutting timber in Canaan Valley. A year later he moved more than 700,000 feet of logs to a storage dam [splash dam] just above Davis, via the Blackwater River.

A photo of the dam creating the storage pond [splash dam] in Canaan Valley that became the object of growing hostility between Robert Eastham and the Thompsons. The dam was built entirely of logs and covered in wood planks with stone piles on each side of the river to secure it to the force of the water pressing on the dam. This dam was located on the Blackwater River near the center of Canaan Valley and its remnant stone piles and a few decaying logs can still be seen today. Photo courtesy of Ruth Cooper Allman.

In June 1887 Robert Eastham became one of the founding stockholders of the Blackwater Boom and Lumber Company. One year later the company was sold to a trio of investors including Albert Thompson. Thompson became the company's manager. By 1890 Eastham's business ventures were slowing. He did contract with Thompson to cut timber on his own nineteen hundred acre tract of land in Canaan Valley. However, by the summer of that year he sold his holdings in Davis and Canaan Valley and moved back to his hometown in Virginia. This departure was short lived, and he returned to the Davis area a year later. Eastham again purchased land in Canaan Valley and made a deal with the Blackwater Boom and Lumber Company to cut the timber.

Bad Economic Times

As a result of the continued downturn in the economy, Blackwater Boom and Lumber Company was declared insolvent in March 1893. Eastham was forced to accept a settlement for his timbering venture that was distasteful to him. One month later, the company was sold to William Osterhout for $110,000, with $25,000 due immediately. Albert Thompson and his son Frank provided the money. An angry Eastham and his partner were the loosing bidders.

The company emerged as the Blackwater Lumber Company, with Albert's son Frank serving as manager, vice president and treasurer. One of the tasks facing the new company was getting the estimated sixteen miles of lumber in the Blackwater River to the mill in Davis. While logs were being moved to Davis from Canaan Valley by train, many more were being added to the river from timber operations, at a rate faster than the mill could process. This back up in the river was also a problem for Eastham's logging enterprise. In the winter of 1893-94, Eastham cut timber on a tract he was managing. Approximately one thousand cords of pulpwood were placed in the river that spring. By January 1895, Eastham threatened to "open up the river" if the blockade was not broken. By the end of that month an agreement was reached. The agreement put much of Eastham's pulpwood on railcars and delivered it to the West Virginia Pulp

A photo portrait of Robert Eastham (above), possibly taken at a studio in Davis or Thomas, near Canaan Valley. Eastham was a physically large and imposing individual and here he seems determined to ensure this likeness of him captures that character. This photo appeared in *Mosby's Rangers: A Record of the Operations of the Forty-Third Virginia Battalion Virginia Calvary from Its Organization to the Surrender*, by James J. Williamson, and published by Ralph B. Kenyon, New York, 1896, page 372.

and Paper Company in Davis.

The river remained blocked well into the summer of 1895. Earlier in the spring, someone had opened the storage pond allowing thousands of logs to escape. Obviously, Eastham was suspected but was never charged. In May, the Blackwater Lumber Company won a temporary injunction against Eastham preventing him from interfering with the company's storage ponds along the Blackwater River. This action seemed to add fuel to an already volatile situation. Over the next four months a hole was dynamited in a storage pond, several attempts to make repairs were stopped by gunfire and the storage pond was eventually destroyed by fire. Eastham had earlier claimed control of the storage pond because it was located on property he was logging. In late 1895 the Thompsons were able to purchase this piece of property, thus putting an end to any possible control of the dam. The Blackwater Lumber Company began to prosper over the next several years. A turn around in the economy allowed for a major increase in their land holdings in the area. Eastham's disdain for the Thompsons also increased.

March 18, 1897

Eastham circulated a petition blasting a judge's ruling against one of his friends. The judge ordered the petitioners to appear at the county courthouse, in Parsons, on charges of contempt. Frank Thompson was at the courthouse when the judged fined only four of the sixty-five petitioners. Eastham was one of the four. At the West Virginia Central and Pittsburg depot in Parsons, Eastham had arranged for a single railcar to return his party back to Davis. Frank Thompson somehow had purchased a ticket for the return trip on the train. His presence infuriated Bob Eastham. The story goes that after being told to get off the train and being struck across the face by Eastham, Thompson rose and drew a pistol. Several passengers warned Eastham, who drew and shot Frank Thompson three times. Thompson was able to get off several shots but only grazed Eastham. Severely wounded, Thompson was taken off the train to a nearby motel. There he was treated by a doctor but later sent by a special train to Cumberland,

This photo, left, of Frank Thompson appeared in the August 28, 1958 issue of The Parsons Advocate as part of a lengthy article by Tucker County historian Homer Floyd Fansler detailing the story of the murder of Thompson by Robert Eastham. Fansler's account of the lives of the two men is particularly interesting in that it is a less than glowing commentary on the character of Eastham. Fansler says, "Eastham was always in trouble."

Behold! The Land of Canaan

Maryland. Surgery was performed, but Thompson died two days later on March 20, 1897. Eastham was arrested on March 22 and taken to the Tucker County jail where he was denied bail and remained for the next nine months until his trial.

The Trial

Judge Homer Holt, the same judge who earlier fined Eastham for contempt, would preside over the case. The judge voided the recommendations of two grand juries indictments for manslaughter. The third grand jury returned an indictment for murder. During the trial, Eastham claimed he fired in self defense. After the testimony of sixty-two witnesses, the question of who fired first was never answered beyond a reasonable doubt.

The jury found Eastham guilty of a misdemeanor, manslaughter, and sentenced him to serve an additional fourteen months in the county jail. Surprisingly, less than three months later Eastham walked out of the jail with the assistance of many supporters, including the jailer. Robert Eastham returned to his home in Rappahannock County, Virginia, where he lived for the next twenty-six years. Molly Eastham died near the end of World War I, and Robert married Bessie Jordan. At age 82, Eastham had a stroke while riding his horse and died on April 9, 1924.

Sources

"Bob Ridley Eastham: Ranger Who Followed Trail of Adventure, Robert Eastham." The Rappahannock News 29 December 1893 and 5 January 1984.

Guthrie, Keith. "Logging in Canaan: The Triumphs and Tragedy of a Tucker County Timber Baron." A Bit of Canada Gone Astray - Canaan Valley. Canaan Valley Institute. Davis, WV: McClain Printing Co., 2002.

Maxwell, Hu. "History of Tucker County." Kingwood, WV: Preston Publishing Co., 1884. Reprinted Parsons, WV: McClain Printing Co., 1971, 1993.

"On Trial for His Life." The Parsons Advocate 3, 10, 17 December 1891.

ca. 1920s

2009

THE PARSONS DEPOT

The railroad depot in Parsons, scene of the Frank Thompson shooting, was built in 1889 at a cost of $1300. The photo above is from an undated postcard and was probably taken in the 1920s as evidenced by the size of the trees. Passenger service through Parsons served the citizens of Tucker County for nearly sixty years, ending in 1958. The depot was added to the National Register of Historic Places in 1996. Today, the Parsons Depot is known as the Heritage House and is a center for local artists to display and sell their wares. It is also a museum for historical railroad memorabilia related to the heyday of railroading in Parsons and surrounding areas of Tucker County.

"Ab" Crossland

The Moonshiner Who Beat City Hall

You can't fight City Hall! Most of us have heard that old expression, but I'd like to share a story with you about an exception to that rule which occurred here in a remote part of West Virginia called Canaan Valley. Albert "Ab" Crossland is our celebrity from the late 1960's in this story. He fought the State of West Virginia over the issue of Squatter's Rights-- and won!

Ab Crossland was born on May 17, 1884 in Grant County, West Virginia, the ninth of ten children born to George T. and Provey Jane Yoakum Crossland. George T. was born in 1838 in Huddersfield, England and came to America in 1861, where he joined General George McClellan's Union Army as a mercenary soldier. He was transferred to what is now Tucker County, West Virginia and took part in the Battle of Corricks Ford, where General Garnett was killed, making him the first general who perished in the war between the states. George was honorably discharged from the Union Army on May 14, 1865 at Harpers Ferry and then moved to Grant County and eventually to the southern end of Canaan Valley in the 1890s.

Ab lived all of his adult life in Canaan Valley and was a neighbor of the Joe Heitz family Ab and Joe Heitz manufactured "moonshine"

Left to right: Ab Crossland, Joe Heitz, Sr., Jake Harr, young John Cooper, Joe Heitz, Jr., around 1910. Photo courtesy of Hallie Warner Brenwald, granddaughter of Joe Heitz, Sr.

liquor and had an excellent marketing venue at a local dance hall called The Platform, which was located very close to their residences. The Platform, which originally consisted of nothing more than a wooden platform for a dance floor, was located on the east side of what is now Rt. 32 in Canaan Valley on the Crossland Farm. Sometime in the 1920s a new dance hall was built across the road on the Harr Farm. This building burned down, and a larger and fully enclosed dance hall was built and operated by the Harr family. This new facility was called the Piney or Pine Ridge and was later purchased and managed by Cecil Goff. As was customary in many rural areas in this region, these dance halls were the center of social life for locals each week.

Joe Heitz, who moved to Canaan Valley in 1898, had seven children, one, Joseph, Jr., known as "Toots" in his adult life, owned a country store as well as a pet bear. Many stories are told of Toots and his bear, especially when he would conduct his "bear chases", which, according to Ruth Cooper Allman in her book, Canaan Valley and the Black Bear, were attended by hundreds of people.

So, between The Platform and other social gatherings such as Toots' bear chases, Ab and Joe had a great outlet for this much desired moonshine, until they got caught. In modern vernacular, you could say Ab "took the rap" and served ninety days in jail, but Joe was not implicated in this crime. In a gesture of appreciation, Joe gave Ab lifelong squatter's rights to erect a cabin and workshop on the property the Heitz family owned.

On returning home after his stay in jail, Ab, with the assistance of Joe, Jr., (Toots) decided to relocate their operation to a much more inconspicuous location up Mill Run in a well-hidden cave. The most advantageous aspect of the new site for their secret moonshine production was the ventilation of smoke from the fires used during their distillation process.

This smoke was drawn into the cave and carried upwards, like a chimney, to be faintly expelled somewhere on the other side of Weiss Knob some five miles away. When the "revenoors" from the Internal Revenue Service would attempt to find Ab and Toots busily making moonshine, they would observe the smoke from the Laneville side of Weiss Knob and search over some rather rough territory. Needless to say, they never found the source of the smoke or found Ab and Toots distilling their moonshine. It is believed by local cavers that the entrance to this cave was excavated shut when the state park did the clearing and construction of one of the ski trails at the Canaan Valley State Park ski area. Local cavers Jim Good and O. B. Collins explored the area around Mill Run and found two caves but not the one used by Ab and Toots.

After the death of Joe, Sr., and later, Joe, Jr., the Heitz family questioned the validity of the squatter's rights given to Ab, but never legally pursued having the rights revoked. The location of this building was on the east side of present day Rt. 32 where the entrance to the Canaan Valley ski area exists today. Ab's home consisted of two box cars, placed on the north side of the ski area access road, and a frame blacksmith shop on the south side.

In 1956, the state received a gift of land from Mrs. Sarah Maude Thompson Kaemmerling, a cousin of George Thompson of Thompson Lumber Company fame, in the amount of 3,149 acres. As a result of this gift, the State of West Virginia established the Canaan Valley State Park in 1964. They began the project by purchasing 34 acres from Ada Harr. Then, through condemnation, West Virginia took 26 farms, homes, and portions of nine other farms between 1965 and 1970. These people had no desire to leave their homes and the lifestyle they had, and the state was offering a paltry sum, which in most cases was much less than it would

Photo taken around 1939 of Joe Heitz, Jr. giving his pet bear a soda pop. Known as "Toots" to family and friends, Joe and his father, Joe, Sr. were partners of Ab Crossland in a moonshine enterprise. Photo courtesy of Nancy Smith Johnson, granddaughter of Toots Heitz.

take for them to relocate. Their only recourse was to plead their case in court, located in Parsons. These cases were presented to their respective juries, many members of which were not from Canaan Valley or nearby areas "on the mountain". These citizens lived a very different life from those in Canaan Valley in the 1960's and had no real grasp of property values for these "condemned" farms.

The judge presiding over these proceedings was Judge D. E. Cuppett who had the reputation of being extremely arrogant and righteous and had no interest in being considerate or compassionate. At the time, a judge's term was twelve years, so the residents and attorneys of Tucker County had no recourse but to plead their cases before him.

When Ab Crossland appeared before Cuppett in court in Parsons, the Tucker County Seat, pleading his case by citing English Common Law on the issue of Squatter's Rights, Cuppett berated Ab and tried to make a mockery of him and the entire judicial process. Two local attorneys who were present in court that day representing clients on other cases and who were knowledgeable about Judge Cuppett and his arrogant ways, took offense to the judge's handling of Ab's case; and with encouragement from Roscoe Beall, Sr., approached the bench, and requested a recess to discuss this matter with Ab Crossland. On returning, these attorneys, Ron Brown (later prosecuting attorney for Preston County) and Larry Starcher (later a State Supreme Court Justice of West Virginia) entered a plea on behalf of Ab and were immediately rebuked by Cuppett. These

Ab Crossland in the doorway of his cabin around 1970. Photo by Ruth Cooper Allman for her book, *Canaan Valley and the Black Bear*, reprinted here with her permission.

two lawyers with the assistance of attorney Milford Gibson of Elkins, who was friends with the Heitz family, appealed to the State Supreme Court with additional testimony from the Heitz family as well as Common Law rulings on the issue. All three of these men truly had contempt for Judge Cuppett concerning his conduct in the courtroom that day and decided to fully pursue the case. As a result of their legal actions, the State Supreme Court unanimously ruled in favor of Ab. The decision was handed back to Judge Cuppett, but Cuppett, true to his righteous and arrogant ways, would not admit he was wrong and refused to serve the proper and legal papers on Ab.

The end result was that Ab was never served the papers that stated his Squatter's Rights had been upheld or that the State could legally purchase his property. So, Ab continued to live on his place until his death on April 4, 1973. In addition, other local families, had had their land taken away through the condemnation process, and had no recourse but to move away.

The location of Ab's "shacks" was a significant issue for the State Park's hierarchy, for he was planted right along the road leading to the ski area which the Park was constructing. One

Photo of Ab's cabin that appeared in the April 12, 1970 issue of the Morgantown Dominion Post as part of an article written by Jim Stacy about Ab's legal battles with the state.

Behold! The Land of Canaan

of the more amusing stories arising from this era was that when State Park employees would approach Ab in his cabin, he would meet them at the door, shotgun in hand, telling them to get off his property and proceed to bang the butt of his gun on the floor, causing his pet skunks to greet the visitors with their tails held high. Ab did this because his attorneys had informed him of the Supreme Court's decision and he knew what his rights were. After a few of these encounters, the uninvited intruders ceased to harass Ab and left him alone.

As the opening of the Canaan Valley Ski Area (Winter, 1971-72) grew closer, news of Ab's legal battle began to spread. Articles describing the proceedings appeared in The Washington Post and Grit newspapers. Ab Crossland became somewhat of a celebrity for winning his legal battle on the grounds of Squatter's Rights, a decision not very common here in the East in the late 1960's. Ab received quite a lot of correspondence due to his notoriety and even some offers of matrimony!

Ab lived another four years after all the legal wrangling ceased, but he was in failing health for the last year of his life. During this time Lester "Buck" Hinkle of Hinkle Funeral Home in Davis would transport Ab in his ambulance to the emergency room or doctor and never charge him a cent. Ab confided in Buck, and eventually they became close friends. Ab requested that Buck take care of his funeral arrangements and settle his estate in the case of his passing, which occurred April 4, 1973. Ab was buried next to his mother in a family cemetery on state park property, which once belonged to the Crossland family.

Buck Hinkle arranged

and advertised an auction that would sell Ab's belongings as well as the buildings that he occupied with the stipulation that all items be removed within thirty days of the sale. On a local note, Jim Good and David "O.B." Collins purchased the blacksmith shop, which was constructed of solid chestnut lumber and "recycled" the lumber as paneling in their residences.

Many items of interest would be auctioned, such as bear traps, hand tools, and other things that any mountain man would possess, but the big draw, Buck figured, would be Ab's moonshine still, or at least one of them. This, indeed, drew interest, especially from agents from the IRS who were assigned the task of preventing the manufacture and sale of moonshine. The biggest issue concerning the "revenoors," as they were called, was that this

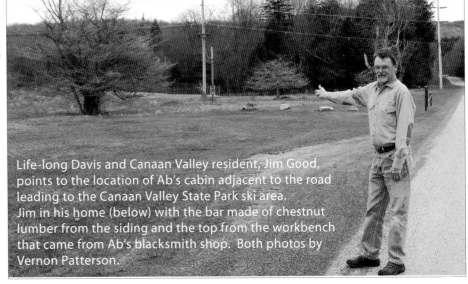

Life-long Davis and Canaan Valley resident, Jim Good, points to the location of Ab's cabin adjacent to the road leading to the Canaan Valley State Park ski area.
Jim in his home (below) with the bar made of chestnut lumber from the siding and the top from the workbench that came from Ab's blacksmith shop. Both photos by Vernon Patterson.

liquor, usually rather potent, was being sold without any tax being collected. One could imagine that guys like Ab Crossland and Toots Heitz didn't think that any government agent had any business eating into the profits of their labor.

Prior to the auction of Ab's belongs and buildings, either Buck Hinkle or a State Park employee decided to incapacitate the still by drilling holes in the metal. When this item was brought forward for auction, the attending IRS agents observed the holes and declared the still inoperable and, therefore, promptly left satisfied that this still could never produce any illegal, untaxed liquor again. On observing the departure of the revenoors, Buck then auctioned off a full box of rivets, which any good sheet metal man would know were for repairing holes in almost any kind of metal including a mash cooker full of holes. It just goes to show that not only can a good moonshiner beat city hall, he can beat those danged revenoors too.

Photo of Ab being given a tour of the new state park ski area during opening ceremonies in 1971. Other person is unidentified. Photo courtesy of Alpine Festival, Davis, WV.

Acknowledgements

The author would like to extend special thanks to the following individuals for their time in providing their recollections and information vital to telling Ab's story: Ronnie Beall, Clyde Crossland, Jim Good and Dick Harr. Also to Emily Warner Smith and Hallie Warner Brenwald for their recollections Joe Heitz, Jr. and Joe Heitz, Sr., Special thanks also to Linnie Spence for assistance as scribe and editor and to Vernon Patterson for photography.

Photo of Ab's grave next to that of his mother Provey "Poppy" Yoakum Crossland (1843-1901). The site of the original Cabin Mountain Ski Area can be seen in the background. Photo by Vernon Patterson, April 2010.

Behold! The Land of Canaan

Obituaries

ALBERT LEWIS CROSSLAND

Albert Lewis Crossland, 88, of Davis died April 4 in Tucker County Hospital, Parsons.

Mr. Crossland was born in Grant County on May 17, 1884, a son of the late George T. and Provie Yokum Crossland.

He is survived by one brother, Nile Crossland, of Eglon; one half sister, Mrs. Martha Lewis of Parsons; several nieces and nephews. Five brothers and four sisters are deceased.

Graveside rites were conducted April 6 in the Crossland Cemetery in Canaan Valley. Hinkle Funeral Home in Davis was in charge of the arrangements.—The Parsons Advocate 4-11-73

Obituary courtesy of Virginia (Cooper) Parsons.

"I remember Ab well, and the pictures of him [in this story] are just as I remember. I spent a lot of time at my grandparents' home since it was just across the highway from our home, and many nights when I "slept over" there, Ab would come to watch TV for the evening. With a Burnside stove for heat, the room was very warm, and the odor from Ab's layers of clothes would get pretty bad. My grandma and I would retire to the kitchen and find a cooking project or something to do and leave Toots in the dining room where the TV was located to watch TV with Ab! He would stay until 10 or 11 pm, depending what was on TV, and then get his flashlight out for the walk home. He was quite an interesting character.

An interesting note for my husband and I is that we got engaged on Thanksgiving day of 1965, while taking Ab's Thanksgiving dinner to him. My mother got things together to take to Ab after we ate dinner, and Bob Johnson, my then boyfriend, offered for us to take the meal. When we returned home, I had a diamond engagement ring on my left hand! So, I guess I can say, thanks to Ab, I have had a wonderful marriage for 44 years!"

A FINAL NOTE...Nancy Smith Johnson, granddaughter of Joe Heitz, Jr., recalls Ab Crossland

Ab Crossland's father George Thomas "G.T." Crossland (1838-1931) was born in England. He came to America and fought on side of Union in the Civil War, including the Battle of Corricks Ford. G.T. first married Provey Jane "Poppy" Yoakum (1843-1901). G.T. and Provey were the parents of ten children: Selena, Edward, Victoria, Syminthy, Elizabeth, Thomas, William, Howard, Albert, Nile. Provey was buried in Crossland Cemetery in Canaan Valley. After Provey's death, G.T. married Clara Burdette. He is buried in the Parsons City Cemetery. Photos courtesy of Rita Anne Judy Raines-Lambert (granddaughter of Ab's brother, Thomas Jefferson Crossland).

Miss Bessie Harr Weds Canaan Valley Farmer
A Local, Long Ago Love Story

The author Debra Lucille Harr, daughter of E. Debs and Lucille "Tippy" Harr and niece to Victor and Bessie Harr Wolford, was born and raised in Petersburg, West Virginia. She and her brother Gene spent plenty of time on the Wolford farm in Canaan Valley as children and young adults. The story title is a headline taken from a 1942 newspaper article announcing the marriage of Bessie Harr and Victor Wolford. Much of the content is taken from her mother's account of the Harr family, "Lest We Forget", written in 1983-84, complemented by Debra's personal recollections.

In 1942 on New Year's Day, Bessie Carrol Harr married her boyfriend, a forty-three year old bachelor named Victor Wolford of Canaan Valley. Vic was the son of Floyd Wolford and Ida Raines Wolford and the grandson of John T. and Narissa Raines Wolford who were married in 1858. He had three sisters: Ada, Ruth and Rose, and four brothers: Amby, Frank, Burrell and Tom. The eighty-five acre farm he and Bessie lived on actually belonged to Vic's parents, as they were heir to this property that sat close to the present day Canaan Valley State Park lodge. Vic had numerous jobs. He was a carpenter, having worked in the position at Blackwater Falls State Park lodge; a mechanic, having worked for Bretherd Chevrolet in Petersburg; a bus driver, with a run from Petersburg to Cumberland with

Meyer Bus Line; but mostly, he was a Canaan Valley farmer.

Bessie Harr Wolford, known to family as "B", attended the Harr School in Canaan Valley, a one room school that was close to the home where she was raised. She was the daughter of John Rufus and Delarie Virginia Hanger Harr of Canaan Valley. "B" was a school teacher in Petersburg in Grant County, West Virginia, at the time of her marriage to Vic. After marriage, Vic joined her in Petersburg for short periods of employment; but, overall, farm management necessitated that Vic return to the Valley full time.

Vic had a soft personality, despite his sometimes distancing comments. He affectionately called his wife "Bess". He refused to acknowledge that he was a sick man at the young age of sixty-one and would not accept traditional medicine offered him. He moved into the Debs Harr home (Bessie's brother) in Petersburg in 1960 where Debs, his wife "Tippy" and Bessie cared for him. Vic died of lung cancer on November 4, 1960, at the Grant County Hospital in Petersburg.

Looking back on his days in Canaan Valley, consider that Vic lived alone on the farm in winter months while Bessie taught in Petersburg. Those days were marked with woodcutting for the wood burning stove in the kitchen and managing livestock–at least one cow, chickens, sheep and some hogs. Snow drifts in the lane to Route 32 often kept him isolated from his friends, family and neighbors for months at a time. In the 1950's a snowy television broadcast of "Sky King" and "Roy Rogers" on a Sunday afternoon in his living room was all that you could make out on the

Bessie Harr celebrates her 70th birthday in 1974 at the vacation home of her nephew Gene Harr in Canaan Valley. Left to right are siblings Dorothy, Debs, Bessie and Hester Harr, all children of John and Delarie Hanger Harr. Gene's vacation chalet was just a short distance from Bessie's new home at the corner of Cortland Road and Maple Grove Lane in Canaan Valley. Photo courtesy of Debra Harr.

television screen. There was country music from a whistling radio that was broadcasting from a Wheeling, West Virginia radio station. A single bulb from the ceiling was light in the barn.

He was a special kind of man who survived these winters and was always there in spring when the Harr family drove out to deliver Bessie at the end of the school year to the damp and snow-crusted soggy bottom that landscaped their home. There, crocus followed by iris of deep purple eventually made their way to full bloom. They still bloom today in that very place.

Summer was extra busy at Vic and Bessie's farm. Vic and Bessie had livestock, sold dairy products and grew cauliflower for Birdseye Vegetable Products of Pittsburgh, Pennsylvania. Bessie canned their garden vegetables and chicken and made homemade butter. They sold milk and eggs. There was the practice of hiring young boys to help in putting up hay. One young man was Wayne Spiggle (now Dr. Wayne Spiggle) whose family owned a local funeral home. Sunsets on the porch after dinner were always warm and refreshing as the breeze blew through the leaves. At night an occasional bear and many deer grazed the field above the house. There were some visitors: Vic's brother Tom Wolford; the Raines family; and Hoy Smith and his wife Louise came often. There was quiet and peace on this farm as Mother Nature with her magnificent beauty graced the landscape through summer, fall and into the snow white of winter. As years passed, they took in hunters and gave them lodging and food during deer season. Many hunters were from Ohio. The Wolford's also had a Christmas tree farm on the property at one time.

After Vic's death, Bessie sold the livestock and returned to Petersburg as the High School

The John Rufus Harr family circa 1920. From left to right: Bessie, Dorothy, Hester, father John Rufus Harr, brother Guy and mother Delarie Hanger Harr; brother Eugene Debs Harr in front. Delarie Harr died six years later, leaving John to manage the rearing of the last of his children, the youngest of which was the author's father Debs, who was twelve years old when his mother died. Photo courtesy of Debra Harr.

Victor and Bessie trimming and boxing cauliflower grown on their farm around 1950. During the 1940s and early 1950s, local Canaan Valley farmers tried to make cauliflower into a cash crop but gave it up in a few years because it was too labor intensive. In this photo, the cauliflower has been hauled to a makeshift workbench where they are using knives to cut off the longest leaves to expose the head inside, then crating it for overnight shipment to market. Photo courtesy of Debra Harr.

librarian and Elementary School teacher through 1964. She was an exemplary teacher and was recognized locally for her many years of devotion to the education of young children. She was the only Harr sibling to have gained a four-year college education. She periodically would return to Canaan and the farm she loved and engaged in pre-retirement life. She rented her chicken house out to a friend who wanted to raise rabbits, and she had a vegetable and flower garden.

In early to mid 1960, she learned to drive a car and bought one of her own. She courted Dr. Feaster Wolford, a relative of Vic's. He was a retired professor of agriculture from Berea College in Kentucky. She was a companion to him for several years. He bought her a ring and their budding relationship was the talk of Canaan Valley–until the tide turned and he found a lady from Kentucky that suited him better.

Bessie was forced to sell the farm in 1967 to become part of Canaan Valley State Park. Helped by her brother Debs and other siblings, there was an auction of all farm machinery and equipment. They even sold the porcelain doorknobs from the house. I recall her last day there: she took Vic's farm hat and her garden bonnet and hung them in the mud room off the kitchen, their usual place, and walked out of the door for the last time.

In short order, the state-owned bulldozer knocked down the house and barn and other outbuildings and burned them. It was the end of a chapter in all of our lives. Fortunately for Bessie, she was able to buy property from Hancel "Hank" and Erma Mallow on Cortland Road in the Valley. There, she built a simple ranch style home where she attended to her flower garden and engaged in sewing and oil painting. She still hosted the Harr family through the years at this new place until she passed away on September 5, 1976. Bessie was buried at Maple Hill Cemetery in Petersburg beside her husband Victor Wolford.

Victor Wolford and his new bride Bessie pose for a picture in the early 1940s at their home on their farm in Canaan Valley. Sitting between them is the author's brother, Eugene Harr. Known as Gene to family and friends, he grew up in Petersburg, West Virginia. Before he passed away in 2000, he provided for a generous donation to the Grant County Library from his estate. In 2007 a new Performing Arts Center was built in Petersburg and its theater was named "The Eugene K. Harr Theatre". Photo courtesy of Debra Harr.

Behold! The Land of Canaan

Victor Wolford and Bessie Harr Wolford Family Tree

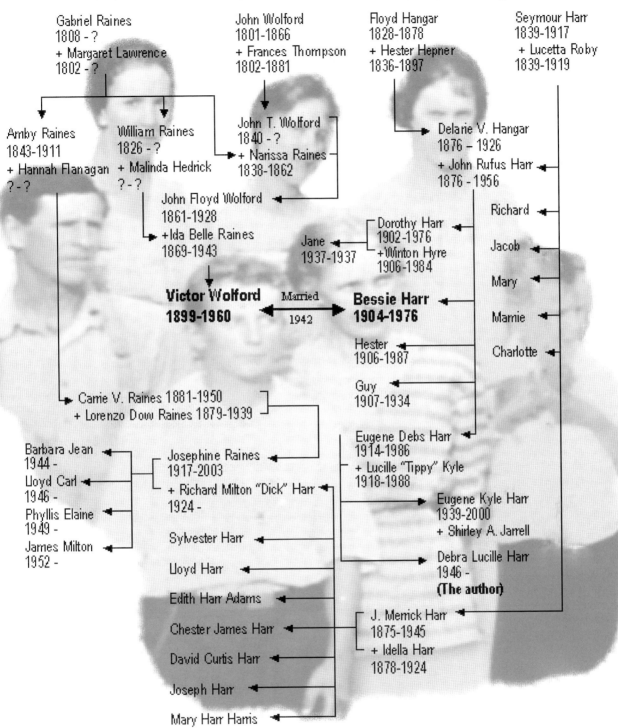

The family tree of the ancestors and descendents of Victor Wolford and Bessie Harr shows its connections to some of the names common in Canaan Valley history–Raines, Flanagan, Hedrick, Roby, Lawrence and others. Victor and Bessie were married later in life and did not have any children of their own, but they often spent time with their nieces and nephews and other members of their family. The genealogical information shown here was assembled from documents provided by Dick and Carl Harr, Juanita Pennington Stewart, Rita Anne Judy Lambert and with additional guidance from Debra Harr.

THE HARR FAMILY'S 130 YEARS IN CANAAN VALLEY

They Came to America 300 Years Ago and to West Virginia 200 Years Ago

The chilly, damp weather seemed to drain the spirit of everyone in the family. And it only added to the stress on the mother of the new baby in the household; oddly, she was not regaining her strength in the weeks following the arrival of her infant. She was no stranger to childbirth and it seemed unusual to her that she continued to feel tired and listless even after six weeks. Despite this, she was still looking forward to being active again with her husband and other children working on their large farm in Canaan Valley. But suddenly on a Saturday morning, she became violently ill and within a few minutes, she died. It was May 31, 1924 and at age 44, Idella Harr left behind a husband to look after their eight children, including two-month old Richard "Dick" Milton Harr.

Today, at age 86, Dick Harr talks about the mother he never knew, his family and roots in West Virginia and all he has witnessed in Canaan Valley over these many years. In several oral history interviews conducted with Dick in the past few years he tells the stories of his life and the tales that were passed to him by his father and others from earlier generations.

From the rich material about the Harr family that Dick provided and from other sources on the Harr family in the deeper past, this account was assembled and is presented here with the family's permission.

The saga of Dick Harr's modern branch of his family tree from which both his mother and father are descended begins well before the American Revolution. Dick's mother, Idella Harr, was the granddaughter of Zimri Harr. Dick's father, James Merrick Harr, was the grandson of Zimri's brother, Merrick Harr. As second cousins, Dick's parents had a common great-grandfather, John Harr, born in 1777, the son of Simon Harr. It is with Simon Harr's life where Dick Harr's story in America on his father's side begins.

Simon Harr, The Great Great Great Grandfather of Dick Harr

Simon Harr was born in Germany in 1734, crossed the Atlantic Ocean on the good ship *Chesterfield*, and arrived in Philadelphia on September 2, 1749. He had just turned fifteen years of age. Family records show that Simon's given name at birth was Hans Jacob Haar, but he later took the name Simon after arriving in America. The family name of Haar was soon anglicized to Harr. When he was 25 years old and still living in Pennsylvania, he married 24year-old Elizabeth Schmitten, also a German immigrant.

Two children quickly arrived for Simon and Elizabeth: Frederick in 1760 and John Henry in 1761; a son Mathias was born in 1767. Mathias was born in Shenandoah County, Virginia, near the town of Strasburg, indicating that the Simon Harr family moved there from Pennsylvania a few years after he was married. But tragedy struck the young family when Elizabeth died in the fall of 1773 at age 38. With three children to look after, thirty-nine year-old Simon wasted little time in finding a new wife and during the following summer he married the widow Eve Printzler. A son John was born to Simon and Eve in 1777 and a son David in 1778. Again tragedy struck and Eve died in 1789 at age 34, and again Simon was left with children to care for. With no lack of haste, Simon married the widow Margaret Baer the following year. No children were born of this marriage and Simon died six years later at age 62.

Simon Harr's life work was dedicated to the Lutheran Church, first in Pennsylvania and later at St. Paul's Lutheran Church in Strasburg, Virginia. There Simon was the schoolmaster for many years. There is no record that Simon was ever an ordained

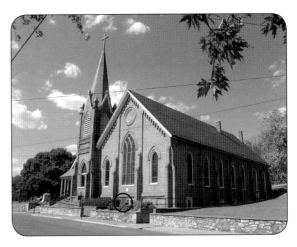

Simon Harr is commemorated on a bronze plaque (circled) in front of beautiful St. Paul's Lutheran Church in Strasburg, Virginia. John Harr, son of Simon and his second wife Eve, moved to present day West Virginia in the late 1700s, and it is from him that the Harr family of Canaan Valley is descended. Photo of plaque courtesy of Bill Watson.

SAINT PAUL'S LUTHERAN CHURCH

HISTORIC VALLEY CONGREGATION, STRASBURG'S OLDEST. ORGANIZED BY GERMAN SETTLERS (C. 1747) WHO FIRST WORSHIPPED IN LOG BUILDING. JUST WEST OF THIS SITE. PARISH RECORDS DATE FROM 1769. STRASBURG'S FIRST SCHOOL CONDUCTED BY THE CONGREGATION AND ITS SCHOOLMASTER, SIMON HARR, FROM 1779 TO 1815.

DURING THE WAR BETWEEN THE STATES, THE BRICK BUILDING ERECTED ON THIS SITE IN 1844 WAS USED BY FEDERAL TROOPS AS A HOSPITAL, ARSENAL, AND STABLE. THE BELL TOWER AND FACADE WERE COMPLETED IN 1893.

PRESENTED BY
LUCY LUDWIG
1961

minister, but he was appointed by the county to perform marriages and records show that he officiated at more than three hundred such events during the last fifteen years of his life. Today, there is a plaque on St. Paul's Lutheran Church in Strasburg commemorating the contributions of Simon Harr in the early years of the church.

Simon had two sons named John, one with his first wife Elizabeth and one with second wife Eve. It is John, son of Simon and Eve, that continued the Harr line that leads us to today's Canaan Valley resident Dick Harr.

John Harr, son of Simon and Eve, was born in 1777, grew up in the area around Strasburg and while he was a young man moved to western Virginia near where Fairmont, West Virginia is located today. He married Elizabeth Merrifield in 1800 and, taking to heart the admonition to go forth and multiply, they had fourteen children over the next twenty-five years. Two years after their last child was born, John Harr died at age 50. His wife Elizabeth lived for another twenty-five years and never remarried. Among the fourteen children of John and Elizabeth Harr were two sons, Merrick and Zimri.

The Brothers Merrick and Zimri Harr

Merrick Harr, son of John and Elizabeth Harr, was born in 1813, the eighth of fourteen children. At age 25, he married Sophia Stark who, over the next ten years, brought

seven of their children into the world. Their first child was Seymour, born in 1839, followed by Priscilla, James, Rufus, John, Louisa, and Jacob. Just five years after Jacob was born, Merrick died at age 40. Sophia lived another twenty years and died at age 62.

Merrick's brother, Zimri, was born in 1823, the thirteenth of John and Elizabeth Harr's fourteen children. He grew up with his many brothers and sisters in the vicinity of Fairmont, West Virginia and that was where he lived his life. In 1848 he married Lavina Barker and they brought eight children into the world over the next fifteen years: John, Eliza Jane, Raleigh, Socrates, David, Richard, Ida and Lucinda. Zimri and Lavina Harr lived their lives in Marion County, not far from Fairmont; Zimri died in 1900 and Lavina in 1904 and both are buried in Marion County.

Zimri Harr's Wife, Lavina Barker Harr and Her Ancestors

Lavina Barker brought very interesting roots of her ancestors into the Harr family when she married Zimri Harr. It is well worth briefly departing from the narrative of the Harr family to explore her lineage. Lavina was the daughter of David Barker and Hannah Morgan. Hannah Morgan was the daughter of Zackquill Morgan. Zackquill was the son of Morgan Morgan. So, let's begin with him.

Morgan Morgan, Dick Harr's great great great great grandfather, was born in Wales in 1688, the second of four children, all sons, of Charles and Susan Morgan. Charles's full name was Charles Morgan Morgan (1635-1720), perhaps explaining the reason for young Morgan Morgan's name. The family name *Morgan* has been traced back at least fourteen generations before Morgan Morgan to the name *Ivor Morgan II* in the area of Glamorganshire, Wales at around 850 A.D.

As so many Europeans did in this time period, young

Highway marker along US Route 11 near Inwood, West Virginia identifying the location of Morgan and Elizabeth Morgan's home in colonial Virginia, now West Virginia. Photo courtesy of waymarking.com

Behold! The Land of Canaan

Morgan Morgan immigrated to America in 1712 and first settled in the village of Christiana, Delaware (today, a southern suburb of the city of Wilmington). His three brothers remained in Wales and lived out their lives there. In Delaware, Morgan met and married Catherine Garretson (1693-1773) in 1714, then later found his way to the British colony of Virginia in what is today Berkeley County, West Virginia. Some historians credit him with being the first settler of European descent to live in what is now West Virginia. Morgan and Catherine Morgan moved to the Shenandoah Valley of Virginia at a time when it was virtually uninhabited by settlers. There is a Harr family legend that they spent the first winter in a hollowed out tree trunk before building a home there in 1726. The location of their home is now a national historic site located on old US Route 11, south of the town of Inwood, just inside the West Virginia line.

Morgan and Catherine had eight children, the seventh born of which was a son, Zackquill (1735-1795) named for Morgan's brother Zackquill, Bishop of Cardiff, who remained in Glamorganshire, Wales. Zackquill grew up in the wide open spaces of his father's large land holdings in northern Virginia. He married 20 year-old Nancy Paxton in 1760 and was soon father to three girls: Nancy, Temperance and Catherine. Zackquill's wife Nancy suddenly died in 1765 and with three little girls to look after, Zackquill remarried within the year to Drusilla Springer (1746-1796).

In 1767, Zackquill Morgan and his new family moved to a tract of land on Deckers Creek near where it empties into the Monongahela River in the northern part of present-day West Virginia. It was the same site where Thomas Decker and others had established a settlement in 1758, and all but one were killed or captured by Mingo and Delaware Indians the following year. Indian hostilities had quieted by the time they arrived and Zackquill and Drusilla's family prospered in their new location in the wilds of what would become northern West Virginia years later. Their family continued growing, reaching a total of eleven children of their own, the last of which was born when Drusilla was age 44. One of those eleven was Hannah, who married David

Lavina Barker Harr, around 1880, the great granddaughter of Morgan Morgan. She was also Dick Harr's great grandmother on his mother's side. Photo courtesy of Dick Harr.

Barker, and one of their children was a daughter Lavina. Lavina Barker married Zimri Harr and it is she who brought the Morgan blood line into the Harr family. Among their children was Raleigh "Buck" Harr, the father of Dick Harr's mother Idella.

The modern city of Morgantown, West Virginia had its beginning in 1785 when the Virginia General Assembly approved a request from Zackquill Morgan to survey fifty acres of his land into a town of half-acre lots and to be named *Morgans-Town*. The Morgan family lived there the remainder of their lives; Zackquill died in 1795 and Drusilla in 1796.

The Cousins Seymour and Raleigh Harr

Of John and Elizabeth Harr's fourteen children, Merrick was eighth, born in 1813, and Zimri was thirteenth, born in 1823. The descendents of each of these men became a new branch of the Harr family tree that would eventually come together years later with the marriage of Dick's mother and father.

One branch began with the marriage of Merrick Harr to Sophia Stark and the birth of

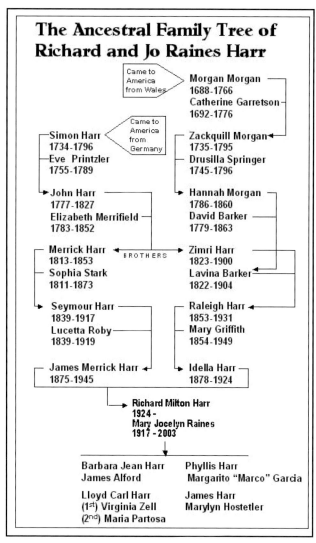

The Ancestral Family Tree of Richard and Jo Raines Harr

Came to America from Wales

Morgan Morgan
1688-1766
Catherine Garretson
1692-1776

Came to America from Germany

Simon Harr
1734-1796
Eve Printzler
1755-1789

Zackquill Morgan
1735-1795
Drusilla Springer
1745-1796

John Harr
1777-1827
Elizabeth Merrifield
1783-1852

Hannah Morgan
1786-1860
David Barker
1779-1863

Merrick Harr
1813-1853
BROTHERS
Sophia Stark
1811-1873

Zimri Harr
1823-1900
Lavina Barker
1822-1904

Seymour Harr
1839-1917
Lucetta Roby
1839-1919

Raleigh Harr
1853-1931
Mary Griffith
1854-1949

James Merrick Harr
1875-1945

Idella Harr
1878-1924

Richard Milton Harr
1924 -
Mary Jocelyn Raines
1917 - 2003

Barbara Jean Harr
James Alford

Phyllis Harr
Margarito "Marco" Garcia

Lloyd Carl Harr
(1st) Virginia Zell
(2nd) Maria Partosa

James Harr
Marylyn Hostetler

The Harr family in Canaan Valley today is only a twig on a branch on a limb of a mighty family tree with members that probably number in the tens of thousands, all descended from Simon Harr and Morgan Morgan. Shown here are the parents, grandparents and beyond of Dick and Jo Harr that carry that blood line back to those two immigrants who came to America in the very early years of America.

their first child, Seymour, born near Fairmont in 1839. At that time, Fairmont was only a little village named Middletown. Seymour's childhood was spent among his parents and siblings on the family farm; he was fourteen years old when his father Merrick died in 1853. From then on it fell upon him to help his mother manage and work the family farm and care for his younger brothers and sisters. The census of 1860 reveals that he was still at home with his mother and siblings when he was 21. There are no records indicating Seymour served in the Civil War, even though he was an ideal age at the time of its outbreak. It is purely speculative but perhaps he was given the choice to remain at home because he was oldest son and the only adult man in the family of his widowed mother and other minor children. Following the Civil War, Seymour married Caroline Reed in 1866, but sadly she died childless the following year. In 1871 he married Lucetta Roby, daughter of Jeremiah and Charlotte Griffith Roby. Seymour was a fairly prosperous farmer and, although he was a teetotaler, he also operated a small distillery. It was a legal business and it is said he made a fine product of distilled spirits from apples that he sold to a local drug store where most medicines available over the counter included a fair share of alcohol. Seymour and Lucetta had seven children, the third of which

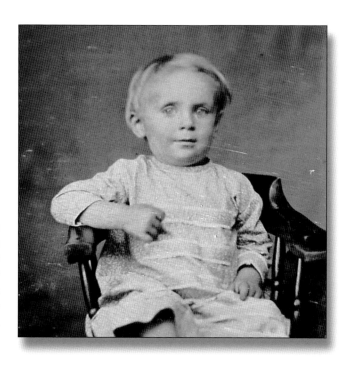

A rare early photo of Seymour Harr taken around 1842. As the son and first child in the family, it is to understand the pride Merrick and Sophia Harr felt and their willingness to undertake the expense of a photograph of Seymour. Photo courtesy of Dick Harr.

Behold! The Land of Canaan

was James Merrick Harr. Known as Merrick to his family, he was the father of Dick Harr.

Dick Harr's mother's branch of the Harr family tree began when Seymour's first cousin Raleigh "Buck" Harr was born in 1853 to Merrick's brother Zimri and his wife, Lavina. By that time, Middletown had become a growing town and was chartered as the city of Fairmont. Raleigh Harr also grew up on his family's farm not far from that of his uncle Merrick Harr. Raleigh, always known as "Buck" to family and friends, was 18 years old when he married 17 year-old Mary Elizabeth Griffith in 1871. Buck and Mary Harr eventually had twelve children, among whom was Idella, the mother of Dick Harr.

Seymour and Buck Harr eventually decided to leave the relative comfort of their lives in the Fairmont area and move to Canaan Valley. Buck and Mary Harr, being the younger of the two couples and perhaps feeling less rooted in the Marion County community, were the first to decide to make the move.

Buck and Mary Harr Relocate to Canaan Valley

In the summer of 1877, Buck and Mary Harr (see "Canaan Valley Settled Just Four Generations Ago", *Chronicles No. 1*, in *Behold! The Land of Canaan 2009*.) sold their farm in Marion County, packed their essential belongings into a horse-drawn wagon and with their children, Warren, Cora and Charles, made the arduous three-day trip to Canaan Valley. When they arrived, they leased a tract of ground from Robert Eastham (see "Robert Eastham, A Transplanted Virginian", page 18) who had arrived in the Valley the previous year. Although there were only one or two families in the Valley at the time, there are clues about where they first lived. When Mary Harr was past 90 years old she related to her family that the first place they lived was "near the cross road that leads to where John Harper lives now". Coincidently, Ruth Cooper Allman tells in an oral history that when her grandfather, Henry Jackson Cooper, and his family arrived in Canaan Valley in 1882, they first lived in the "old Harr house", as they called it. Years later, Ruth says Ben Thompson

once told her that the "old Harr house" was located at the present site of the Canaan Valley Volunteer Fire Department parking lot. At the time Mary Harr told of their first home, around the mid 1940s, Cortland Lane (recently renamed Sagebrush Lane) led almost exactly to the John Harper home (Today the now-vacant Harper home place is opposite Cluss Lumber Company on Cortland Road.) It is quite possible that Buck and Mary Harr built a crude cabin there when they arrived in 1877. Vacating it soon after, it was available for the Cooper's when they arrived in 1882. The Buck and Mary Harr family almost certainly spent the winter of 1877-78 in the old Harr house.

Over the next year or two, according to the account given by the elderly Mary Harr, the Buck Harr family moved several times, first renting a home on the property of William Henry Harrison Cosner, and then later renting in the extreme southern end of Canaan Valley on the property of the Wilmoth family. It was a difficult time for the Harr family. The timber industry had not yet gotten underway and the Valley was nearly covered by a dense forest of huge spruce, hemlock, cherry, beech, poplar and maple. Little food could be grown in a family garden because making a large enough clearing in such a forest to plant crops would have required an enormous amount of work. Buck surely found it far too difficult for a man without a several strong sons to help. The town of Davis did not yet exist and it was a three-day round-trip by horse and wagon to Petersburg or St. George to purchase the most rudimentary supplies of flour, salt, gunpowder, yard goods and other necessities. Buck's skill as a hunter was well known, and he was often gone for days at a time hunting game to feed his family or leading hunting parties from Fairmont to make some much needed extra money. Buck's time away left Mary and the children alone, adding to the hardships she endured in making a home for her family in the Canaan wilderness.

On November 10, 1878, Mary gave birth to Adelia, the first Harr family member born in Canaan Valley. Called variously Idella, Della and Dellie, this little girl would grow up to be the mother of Dick Harr. Ultimately, she was known to nearly everyone as Idella. Baby Idella

Raleigh "Buck" Harr had a reputation among men in Canaan Valley as being a fearless bear hunter. The more often the stories about Buck were told around a woodstove on the cold winter's evening, perhaps aided by a sip or two of moonshine, the more extraordinary his feats became. Lucian H. Mott (1882-1974), a resident of Davis for many years and highly regarded for his integrity and service to the community, wrote and signed a brief story about one of Buck's alleged bare-fisted encounters with a bear. Although the account is considerably less hair-raising than the accounts that circulated about Buck, it was certainly a closer brush with an angry bear than most people wished to experience.

"BUCK" HARR AND
THE BLACK BEAR

Soon after I came to Davis I heard that Raleigh "Buck" Harr had killed a bear with his fist. I was anxious to see the giant who had accomplished such a feat. One day while in his home in the upper part Canaan Valley, I asked Mr. Harr if he really had killed a bear with his fist. The following is what he told me:-

"A man by the name of Swearingen and were out in the woods when we came upon two young cubs. The only tool we had with us was an axe. I told Swearingen to hold the cubs while I cut a club, for the mother bear will soon be coming to her young. I cut a club just the size I wanted and picked out a bare spot which was covered with moss. I told Swearingen to hold the cubs on the side opposite where the old bear would enter the open spot. It wasn't long until I heard the mother bear crushing the laurel and snorting coming for her cubs. Just as she entered the open spot she reared on her hind feet and she came reaching with her front paws and mouth wide open. I intended to knock her out with the first blow but she threw up a front paw which protected her head. She went down on front feet but up she came and all I could do was to swing with all my might and she was down and up as fast as I could swing. I was about out of wind and wondered what would happen when she turned and went back into the laurel. I looked around and Swearingen had got scared and let the cubs go. One had gone into the laurel and the mother bear had got scent of it is why she went back into the laurel. The other cub tried to climb a tree and we caught it and took it home with us. The next winter a bear was killing sheep. We set a trap and caught a she bear which had gray strips of hair along one side of her head and shoulder and I always thought that was the bear where I had broke the skin with my club."
End of quote.
If Mr. Harr, with his great strength, couldn't kill a bear with a club I am sure I wouldn't want to try it.
Respectfully submitted.
L. H. Mott.

was another mouth to feed and the burden to support his family grew even heavier on Buck's shoulders.

It turned out to be more difficult to make a new life in Canaan Valley than Buck had expected. Buck and Mary relocated to Elk Garden, probably in 1879, where coal mining was just getting started. After getting a taste of the life of a coal miner, bent over all day swinging a pick, Buck and Mary soon returned to Canaan. Another son, Frank, was born in 1881. In November 1882, they bought a thirty-four acre tract of land from Robert Flanagan for the sum of $275.00, perhaps saved from his earnings as a coal miner. Dick says he recalls being told that Buck also included a sewing machine in the deal. There was an old log house on the property, and after a little cleaning and repair work, they moved into their new home. Buck and Mary Harr finally had a place of their own in Canaan Valley.

Buck and Mary's life in Canaan did not turn for the better and they soon returned to the Fairmont area as tenant farmers where their son Ole was born in 1885. But still, Canaan beckoned Buck to return and by the end of the following year, they were back on their little farm in Canaan Valley. In December 1885 daughter Carrie was born, followed by Herbert Milton in 1888.

Herbert Milton Harr grew up in Canaan Valley and attended nearby Harr School. He likely divided his time between helping on the family farm and working on local timbering

jobs. In 1915, Herbert married 18 year-old Constance "Connie" Linger, a union that produced a son, Herbert Milton, Jr. in 1917, followed by four daughters, Rebecca, Eleanor, Virginia and Constance. Young Herbert Milton, known as Milton to family and friends, spent a notable career with the West Virginia state parks system. His contributions as an administrator at the park system's headquarters in Charleston brought him the distinction of having the five thousand square-foot conference center at Blackwater Falls State Park named in his honor. After Milton's retirement in the early 1980s, his interest in the history of the state's natural resources brought him to write and publish a book on the history of the Civilian Conservation Corps camps that were built across the state in the 1930s. Milton Harr passed away in 2010.

As the year 1889 broke anew for the Buck Harr family, there was hope for better times ahead. The town of Davis was a growing town and offered most of the necessities of life within

Behold! The Land of Canaan

a few hours ride, rather than a three-day trip to the nearest town as it was when they first arrived in Canaan. Buck and Mary's family had grown to eight children, and the older ones were beginning to help out with household and farm chores. Adding to their brighter prospects was the news that Buck's cousin Seymour and his family had decided to move to the Valley to make a new life. Idella Harr, the future mother of Dick Harr, was now 12 years old. Perhaps now, events in Buck and Mary's life had turned favorable enough for their family to take root in the Valley.

The Seymour Harr Family Joins Buck and Mary's Family in Canaan Valley

Seymour and Lucetta Harr made the decision to move from the comfort of their home in Lumberport, near Fairmont and move to Canaan Valley when they were both fifty years old. On a three-day trip in horse and wagon, they brought all their belongings and their children Jacob, 16, James Merrick, 15, John 13, Mary, 11, Mamie, 9 and Charlotte, 6. Their oldest son Richard had died three years earlier. Seymour's family was probably a little more affluent than the average farmer of that time, thanks to his distillery business. When they arrived in Davis in 1889, they were well suited financially to purchase a farm and settle into making a new home. Seymour also had three strong sons eager to help with the work and no infant children that needed

This map appeared with an article titled, *By-Paths in the Mountains*, by Rebecca Harding Davis, in Harper's Magazine, July 1880, pages 167-185. It shows what was known about Canaan Valley in the late 1870s, about the time Buck and Mary Harr first arrived there. It illustrates the extent to which they were in an uncharted wilderness with none of the towns of Davis, Thomas or Parsons in existence at that time. There are no roads shown in the Valley and the map maker's information about that area is so sketchy, the portrayal of the Blackwater River and Cabin and Canaan Mountains is more based on imagination than survey.

The Milton Harr Conference Center at Blackwater Falls State Park is named for Buck and Mary Harr's grandson Herbert Milton Harr, Jr. who gave a career of service to the West Virginia state park system. Herbert Milton Harr, Jr.'s father and Dick Harr's mother were brother and sister.

Lucetta's constant attention. In many ways, Seymour and Lucetta were much better prepared to face the challenges of a new life in Canaan Valley than Buck and Mary had been twelve years earlier. Their arrival meant there were now two large Harr families in the Valley, each able to lean on the other in difficult times and celebrate with one another in the good.

Seymour, Lucetta and their children probably stayed with Buck and Mary for a short time after they arrived. In October 1889 they purchased two tracts of land from Samuel Shafer. One piece was 312 acres, located in the vicinity of and along Freeland Road, and the other was 35 acres, along what is today Back Hollow Road. He paid a total of $1400 for both parcels. Then, before too much time had passed, Seymour learned of some dreadful news: Samuel Shafer did not own legal title to the 312 acre tract and its sale to Seymour and Mary had been fraudulent. Thus began an odyssey of lawsuits that lasted for years.

Regardless of how the lawsuits would finally be resolved, the Seymour and Buck Harr families moved ahead with their lives in Canaan Valley. Buck and Mary brought four more children into the world in the decade of the 1890s. The first was Baley in 1890, but sadly he only lived a few days. It was Baley's untimely death that moved Buck to set aside a small patch of ground on his farm as a cemetery. Baley Harr was the first to be laid to rest in the Harr Cemetery. Mary was soon expecting another baby, and a healthy baby girl, Odessa, arrived in 1892. Then Brady arrived in 1894 and finally Bertha in 1897. Mary Harr had given birth to twelve children from the time she was 18 years of age until she was age 43. She was a very hardy woman; she lived another fifty years and outlived five of her twelve children.

Many years of living in that old log house passed before Buck and Mary finally built a home of their own on their little farm. Most of their children were grown and gone when Buck undertook the construction of a two-story home around 1910, made from the ample lumber available in the area. Dick recalls that it was a beautiful home, painted white, but it was built of green, wet lumber and when it dried, cracks opened in many of the walls that were

Seymour and Lucetta Roby Harr photographed a few years after they came to Canaan Valley in 1889. Photo courtesy of Dick Harr

Jacob "Jake" Harr as a young man, son of Seymour and Lucetta Harr. Photo courtesy of Dick Harr.

James Merrick Harr as a young man, son of Seymour and Lucetta Harr and father of Dick Harr. Photo courtesy of Dick Harr.

John Rufus Harr as a young man, son of Seymour and Lucetta Harr. Photo courtesy of Debra Harr

Behold! The Land of Canaan

wide enough to see daylight. The windows were double hung with weights and were purchased from Montgomery Ward. They did not fit very well and between the cracks in the walls and leaky window units, he recalls that the house "was cold as a barn" in the wintertime.

More About the Children of the Seymour and Buck Harr Families

Couins Seymour and Buck Harr were fourteen years apart in age. Events in their lives resulted in both beginning their families at about the same time. Seymour's first marriage ended when his wife died childless. Several years passed before he married Lucetta Roby and their first child, Richard, was born in 1871 when Seymour and Lucetta were both thirty-two years old. It so happens that it was also 1871 when Seymour's 18 year-old cousin Buck married Mary Griffith. This coincidence of dates meant that the arrival Seymour's and Buck's children roughly paralleled one another, but because Buck and Mary were so much younger, they had another six children after Seymour and Lucetta's last child was born.

Richard Harr was the first child of Seymour and Lucetta, born in 1871. When he was 15 years old, he and his brothers were playing ball and he was fatally struck in the head with a ball similar to today's baseball. The family was crushed with grief by the accident. Jacob, known as Jake, born in 1873, was second born and James Merrick Harr was third. Known as Merrick to his family, he was born in 1875 and was 14 years old when he first arrived in Canaan Valley. Before too long, he had found a job working in the booming timber industry, teaming with his brothers Jake and John. John was just a year younger than Merrick.

Through most of the decade of the 1890s, all three young Harr men occupied themselves between woods work and helping out on the family farm. Merrick was one of many men who lived the hard working life of a woods worker, known as a *wood hick*. Often away at remote timber camps for days or a week or more at a time, they worked long days, ate plenty of good food to fuel their bodies, and often got overly rowdy when they had a day or two break from work back in town. For many of them, their short time away from the woods sometimes consisted of little more than an overindulgence in two things: women and liquor.

Little is available from family lore of Merrick's life during these closing years of the nineteenth century. What is known is that Merrick became involved with one Jane Wolford and she had a son by him, born on December 31, 1899. Merrick's son Earl Harr grew up with his mother

The John Harr family around 1920. From left to right: Bessie, Dorothy, Hester, father John Rufus Harr, brother Guy and mother Delarie Hanger Harr; brother Eugene Debs in front. Delarie Harr died six years later, leaving John to manage the rearing of the last of his children, the youngest of which was 12 year-old Debs. Everyone in the photo is now deceased. Photo courtesy of Debra Harr, daughter of Eugene Debs Harr.

in nearby Flanagan Hill, helped along by a step father whom Jane later married. Earl remained in the Laneville area all his life and was well known by the Harr family. Much later, in the years that Dick hosted the Harr family reunions, Earl was invited and was pleased to attend. Maybe one or two of the Harr kinfolk raised an eyebrow at this, but Earl certainly was not at fault for who he was. Most others in the family always greeted him warmly. Dick says he was always a good man, a good church man, a hard worker and he lived past age 90.

Merrick's younger brother, John, married Delarie Hanger in 1901 and they had five children; Dorothy (1902-1976), Bessie (1904-1976), Hester (1906-1987), Guy (1907-1934, tuberculosis) and Eugene Debs in 1914-1986). John and Delarie and their children moved from Canaan to Petersburg, West Virginia around 1918. The timber and lumber business was booming there and John was soon the owner of a prosperous lumber mill. Dick recalls hearing stories about Dorothy, Bessie, and Hester coming to stay with his mother and father during the summer while John and Delarie remained in Petersburg with the boys. It was around 1920 and the three girls, all in their teens, loved to get away from living in town and go out into the open spaces of Canaan where they were not under the ever-watchful eye of their mother, Delarie. With a house full of little children at that time, Dick's mother was happy to have the eager girls come to help out, and the girls were happy to use that as an excuse to get away from home for a few days.

Several years after those enjoyable visits with the Merrick Harr family, Delarie took ill and died in 1926. Now the girls had mostly grown into young woman and faced the real task of helping to

look after Eugene, the youngest of John and Delarie's children. Their father, John, eventually remarried but had no more children. As the Great Depression settled over West Virginia and the rest of America in 1930, John's lumber mill was hit hard by the downward spiral of the lumber market. He was left with untold thousands of board-feet of cut lumber that nobody wanted and almost no income to pay debts or employee salaries. His only alternative was to declare bankruptcy, an event in his life from which he probably never recovered emotionally.

Of John and Delarie's five children, only their last born, Eugene Debs (1914-1986), had children that lived to adulthood. Eugene, known as Debs, married Lucille Kyle (1918-1988) and they had two children, Eugene and Debra. Eugene passed away in 2000, leaving his two daughters and his sister Debra as the only surviving members of John and Delarie Harr descendents with the Harr name.

The fifth born child of Seymour and Lucetta was their first daughter, Mary. She was born in 1878 and came to Canaan Valley with her family in 1889. Mary grew up with the family, married Davis resident, Reese Mayle, but she died in childbirth at age 29 and is buried in Cortland Cemetery.

Following Mary, Mamie was the next born of the children. Born in 1880, she was a youngster of nine when she arrived in the Valley, grew into a beautiful young lady and in 1900, she wed George Franklin Cooper, a prosperous farmer in Canaan Valley, ten years her senior. Frank Cooper, as he was known to family and friends, had come to the Valley as a boy in 1882 with his parents, Henry Jackson and Mary Margaret Cooper. By 1901, Frank and Mamie were expecting their first baby but instead, the Harr and Cooper families had to endure another heartbreak;

A portrait studio photo of Mamie Harr about the time she married George Franklin Cooper. Mamie died in childbirth of twins, one of which survived, a son John Cooper, who was mostly raised by the Harr family in Canaan Valley. Photo courtesy of Ruth Cooper Allman.

Behold! The Land of Canaan

Family studio portrait of Raleigh "Buck" and Mary Griffith Harr, taken around 1899 with the three youngest of their twelve children. Left to right, the children are Odessa, Bertha, and Brady. Photo courtesy of Dick Harr.

Mamie suffered through a devastating labor and childbirth of twins and died as a result. On the day of Mamie's funeral, the girl twin also died. Mamie's coffin was opened, the baby laid in her arms, and both buried together in Cortland Cemetery. The surviving twin, a son John, lived and spent many of his growing-up years with the Harr family and came to consider them as much his family as that of his father, Frank Cooper. When John became an adult, he moved to Ohio to find work, married and had three daughters, lived there the rest of his life, died in 1978 and is buried there. (See "Ruth Cooper Allman: Granddaughter of Canaan Valley's Pioneer Cooper Family", in *Behold! The Land of Canaan 2009.*)

The last of Seymour and Lucetta's children was Charlotte, born in 1883. She never married and spent her life working as a nurse in various hospitals in West Virginia, including some part of her career at Hopemont Sanitarium near Terra Alta. She passed away in 1958.

In a interesting footnote on Seymour and Lucetta's children, Jake, the oldest of the three surviving Harr brothers when the family arrived in Canaan in 1889, remained a bachelor for many years, finally marrying 24 year-old Ada Wolford in 1919 when he was 46 years old. They had four children: Fred, Louise, Carney Jackson (Jack) and Betty. Fred and Jack married but had no children and are now deceased. Betty and Louise are still living; Betty had two children and Louise had three.

In contrast to Seymour and Lucetta's children who were all born before the family arrived in Canaan, most of Buck and Mary Harr's children were born after they arrived here. Their first three children, Cora, Warren and Charles were five years, three years and a few months of age respectively, when the family arrived here in 1877. The very difficult life they found in the untamed wilds of Canaan must have been made even more difficult with three little children that required constant care and attention by Mary.

Despite these challenges, first-born Cora lived to adulthood, married Judd Tabor, and died at age 67. Charles, just an infant when he came to Canaan with Buck and Mary, died in 1929 at age 52. Next born was Warren in 1874. He became a school teacher in the Canaan and Flanagan Hill schools, married Katherine Degler from Canaan Valley and had eight children. He died in 1940 and is buried in Westernport, Maryland. His daughter Josephine Harr McBee, now in her 90s, was healthy and robust enough to attend the annual Harr reunion in 2010 and even led an engaging and interesting discussion of her father and her siblings' lives.

Idella was fifth born in 1878, then Frank in 1881. Frank was a farmer and woodsman in Canaan Valley, married Caroline Kesner in 1908, had eight children and he died in 1964. He and Caroline are both buried in Buena Cemetery in Canaan Valley. Ole was next, born in 1883, married Pauline Harper, had four children, died in 1956 and is buried in Davis Cemetery. Herbert was born in 1887, married Connie Linger, had five children, died in 1944 and is buried in Lewisburg, West Virginia. Baley was born in 1890, lived only a few days and is buried in Harr Cemetery in Canaan Valley. Next was Odessa "Dessie" born in 1892, married Albert

Until only recently, the Harr Cemetery sat almost unnoticed along Back Hollow Road in the southern end of Canaan Valley. This little patch of land was set aside by Buck and Mary Harr when their infant son Baley died in 1890. In the years that followed, other members of the Harr family were laid to rest here along with two children of other families in the community. Bertha Harr was the last burial in 1979. The large stone in the center of the photo is simply engraved HARR. The three stones in the lower right are those of Buck, Mary and Bertha Harr.

A ceremony was held at Harr Cemetery in November 2010 to dedicate a sign erected to commemorate its history. The sign was the idea of 95 year-old Mrs. Josephine Harr McBee who also provided the funding for its manufacture and installation. Mrs. McBee is the daughter of Warren Harr, brother of Dick Harr's mother, Idella. Standing left to right in the photo are L. Carl Harr, Mrs. McBee, Mary Ann Imhoff (daughter of Mrs. McBee's sister, Nellie) and Dick Harr. Photos courtesy of Mrs. McBee's daughter, Jean McBee Coviello.

Raleigh Harr was one of the first settlers in Canaan Valley, arriving in 1877 from the Fairmont area of West Virginia. He and his wife Mary traveled by wagon with their three children; the journey took several days.

At the time the "land of Canaan" was total wilderness.

This ground is Buck and Mary's final resting place, along with other family members: a brother and his wife, an infant son, a nephew, two infant grandsons, and three other young children of extended family.

Bertha Harr, the last surviving child of Buck and Mary, is also buried here.

Behold! The Land of Canaan

Norman Smith in 1914, had four children, died in 1960 and is buried in Meadville, PA. Brady was born in 1894, married Margaret Smith, had no children, died in 1969 and is buried in Davis Cemetery. Last born was Bertha in 1897; she lived in the Buck Harr home place with her mother and father most of her life, died in 1979 and was buried in Harr Cemetery, the last person to be laid to rest there. The memory of Bertha burns bright in the minds of many in the Harr family today because of an error in judgment she made in her later years. It is a story worth telling now.

Bertha Harr Searches for Love Only to Find Betrayal

Bertha, the youngest child of Buck and Mary Harr, lived at the home place many years after Buck and Mary died. Known as Berthie to the family, she never married and the family says she was "in love" with a number of men throughout her life, most of whom were usually married. Dick says that when a gas well was drilled on the Harr home place in the early 1970s and then a pipeline laid from there to the main gas line near Buena Church, one of the men working on that job, Alton Skinner, "sweet talked" Bertha into selling the seventy-four acre tract to him for "one dollar", according to the deed in the courthouse today. What is more, she gave Mr. Skinner nearly all the family furniture, household belongings, and many valuable antiques including the family bible. All in the hope of winning his love. In return, Skinner, a married man, promised to take her to Glenville and take care of her the rest of her life. After the sale was executed and Bertha had moved to Glenville, she realized she had made a terrible error in judgment and asked Dick to help her. Dick recalls that Mr. Skinner's concept of "taking care of her the rest of her life" consisted of giving her a small, hot apartment over a garage. During one of Dick's visits, Bertha asked him to get the sheriff and state police after Mr. Skinner for fooling her into giving away her land. Dick subsequently met with the Tucker County prosecuting attorney and was told that there was nothing that could be done. Bertha had made a legal sale to Mr. Skinner and that

was that. Bertha lived out her days in Glenville until she was no longer able to care for herself, and Mr. Skinner arranged for her to move to a nursing facility in Elkins. She died there in 1979. To this day, the Harr family members aware of what happened have about equal amounts of outrage at Bertha for allowing herself to be duped by Mr. Skinner and likewise at Skinner for having the audacity and arrogance to take advantage of a vulnerable old woman. Skinner died in 1991 and ownership of the land passed to his three adult children who sold it for more than $200,000 in 1993. The last evidence of the Buck and Mary Harr home place was erased when the home and outbuildings were torn down and removed in 2002. Had all of this not happened, this beautiful tract of land would have most likely passed to the Harr family for their use and investment today.

James Merrick Harr and Idella Harr Marry and Begin Their Lives Together

Returning once more to the life of Dick's parents, Merrick was a youngster of fourteen when he came to Canaan in 1889. But Idella Harr was born in Canaan in 1878, only months after Buck and Mary Harr first settled here. If she had a middle name, it is unknown to any of the Harr family today. Her growing up years would have been very unlike those of Merrick; while he was learning skills of hunting, farming, caring for animals and the like, she would have been gaining mastery of the tasks needed to be a successful wife and mother in the West Virginia wilderness. One of those tasks would certainly have been caring for her younger brothers and sisters, at least a half dozen of which followed her in the birth order.

As children growing up, Merrick and Idella were probably well acquainted with one another. They were members of the only two Harr families in Canaan Valley and surrounding areas. Their families lived only a short walk from one another, and often worked together or socialized of an evening or a Sunday afternoon. In these surroundings, the stage was set for Merrick and Idella to be joined in a manner more lasting than living their lives as second cousins.

By the time they became young adults, Merrick and Idella had undertaken more than a passing notice of one another and began spending time together when they could. Any talk of marriage, however, was met with opposition from some of the others in the family, but particularly from Idella's father, Buck Harr. Despite that, they seemed happy to follow their hearts in that regard and in 1901 they were married. Merrick was 26 and Idella 23.

The young couple set up housekeeping in an old log house on a large farm not far from the both of their home places. Court cases and appeals related to the fraudulent sale of a farm in the Valley in 1889 to Merrick's father, Seymour, by Samuel Shafer had been plodding along for more than ten years and it was becoming evident that the matter would soon be settled by Mr. Shaffer being ordered to convey his nearby 276-acre farm to Seymour and Lucetta Harr, the very place where Merrick and Idella had chosen to live. This outcome was exciting news to the Harr's. And before long, there was also exciting news that Idella was expecting a baby; in 1903 a son, Sylvester, was born to the new couple. Despite the concerns of some in the family, Sylvester, later known as Vester to everyone, was a perfectly fine and normal baby, not 'born with a tail" as Granddaddy Buck had ominously warned. As the Harr family rejoiced at the arrival of Merrick and Idella's first baby, they grieved at the loss of another baby in the family. Idella's brother Warren and his wife Katy lost their baby son, Stuart, shortly after he was born; he was the second to be buried in the Harr Cemetery, joining Baley who lay there alone for the previous thirteen years. A year later, Warren and Katy lost still another baby son, Morgan, and he joined Stuart as the third occupant of the Harr Cemetery.

But among these disappointments and grief borne by the Harr families, more good news arrived in 1905 when Merrick and Idella brought into the world another healthy son, Lloyd Hansford. He was known as *Hank* all his life. With his family growing, Merrick worked at as many paying jobs as he could find. As he had done in the years before his marriage, Merrick worked in the woods with his brothers John and Jake and continued to do so for many years that followed. Between timbering jobs and whenever they could find time, all three men also worked their farms for their families' needs.

The Harr Family Finally Takes Ownership of a Grand Canaan Valley Farm

In 1906, the legal proceedings at long last came to a close that had begun fifteen years earlier over the fraudulent sale of more than three hundred acres by Samuel Shafer to the Harr brothers' father, Seymour. After multiple court cases and appeals, in the end, Samuel Shafer was ordered by the court to convey 276 acres of beautiful Canaan Valley farm land that he *did legally own* to Seymour and his three sons, Merrick, John and Jake. This wonderful victory for the Seymour and Lucetta Harr family and their children gave them a superb piece of farmland that would become the home of several generations of the Harr family to come. This was the farm Merrick and Idella had been living on since they were married and now it was now irrevocably jointly owned by Seymour and his sons.

But for Seymour, now age 67 and still anguished over the decision he had made to come to Canaan years earlier, this triumph seemed to come too late. In his latter years, he came to regret making the move to Canaan because he had learned that the farm he sold in the 1880s was found to have good deposits of coal beneath it. As an elderly man, it saddened the family to see him go about his property "divining" for coal in the same way some are said to be able to divine for water. Seymour lived for another ten years after the court decision in his favor but they were years mainly filled with unhappiness and worry.

In 1908, Merrick and Idella's third child, Edith, was born. By this time, Merrick's brother Jake had also moved onto the farm with Merrick and his family. John and Delarie and their growing family were living with Seymour and Lucetta at the home place on which they had resided for most of the previous twenty years. As if the spirits knew Merrick needed sons to help care for the big farm, the next three children he and Idella brought to the world were boys. James

"Jimmie" was born in 1912, David in 1915 and Joseph in 1918.

To some, Jimmie Harr might have been the black sheep of the Merrick and Idella Harr children. He left home at a young age and enlisted in the US Marine Corps and spent a career in the service. He rarely came back to Canaan to visit the family. But Dick does remember one visit Jimmie made back to Canaan. It was about 1933 and Dick was living with his Grandmother Mary Harr and his Aunt Bertha at the Buck Harr home place. Bertha decided she and Dick should drive one of their cows over to a neighbor's farm to be bred to their bull. It was summertime and Dick was always barefoot, and during that walk on those gravel roads, he got a stone bruise on the bottom of his foot. The bruise worsened and filled with puss in a few days and he had become immobilized from going anywhere on foot. It was at this time that Jimmie was back visiting and he told Merrick he knew how to treat Dick's infected foot. So, with Merrick holding Dick down, and Dick screaming and hollering, Jimmie lanced it open, cleaned it out, and bandaged it. In a few days, Dick was well on his way to recovery and out and about once again in his bare feet. From Dick's recollection of that single episode, Dick thinks Jimmie must have been a medic in the Marines. And a good one too. Dick never saw Jimmie again after that. Jimmie died in 1950 and some in the family think alcohol may have been a contributing factor.

David was the next born of Merrick and Idella's children, coming into the world in 1915. Dick's account of him was that he was very likable and good looking, and if he could, sometimes seemed very capable of finding a way to avoid work. And he was also the only one of the Merrick Harr children that finished high school. Known by his middle name, Curtis, to family and friends, he was 9 years old when his mother Idella died and not long thereafter went to live with his older brother, Sylvester, who had already left home at that time. Dick recalls Curtis worked in the Civilian Conservation Corps in Berkeley County, West Virginia in the 1930s, and while he was there, met and married a young lady from the eastern panhandle of West Virginia. Curtis had a career that was involved

with America's growing aircraft industry, working in Ohio and later in Florida. In Florida, he had a daughter but little is known of her by the Harr family in Canaan today.

Next born after Curtis was Joseph in 1918. Dick Harr says it was he and his brother Joe that worked so hard for years to turn the 276-acre farm from a weedy and brushy tract of ground into a superb working farm in the years after World War II. Then in 1920, Mary Opal was seventh born to Merrick and Idella. She was always known as Opal but said she disliked the name because it was the name of a foolish character in one of the newspaper comics. Opal spent most of her adult life in the Harrisonburg, Virginia area working at a hospital. She married, had two children, but at mid life in the 1960s, was struck down with cancer.

Dick Harr, Last Born of Merrick and Idella, Enters Life's Stage

Richard Milton Harr was born on April 14, 1924, the last born of Merrick and Idella's eight children. As was normally the case in those days, he was born at home with Idella assisted by a local midwife. At that time in Canaan Valley, Elizabeth Cosner Harr assisted Idella with Dick's birth. Known as Aunt Bettie to everyone in the Harr family, she was the fourth born of Solomon and Catherine Schell Cosner's ten children. Sol and Catherine had come to Canaan Valley in the 1860s and are credited with being the first permanent settlers here. "Aunt Bettie" was the wife of Buck's brother, Socrates and was widely known and respected in the community as a capable midwife. She was 68 years old when Dick was born, died four years later and is buried in Harr Cemetery.

As revealed in the opening paragraphs of this story, Idella Harr died suddenly about six weeks after Dick was born. At the time she died, Idella's cause of death was attributed to a heart attack, according to a local doctor at that time. Years later, Dick's daughter Phyllis had a chance discussion with a physician about what was known of the circumstances of Idella's death. Based on those sketchy details, the doctor speculated that it was probably a blood clot that broke loose and went to her heart that took her life. Such was the hazards of childbirth and post-natal care at that time.

In the midst of Merrick's grief at the loss of his wife, the demands of his farm and family continued without letup. In addition to Dick, three other children, Curtis, Joe, and Opal, were all under age ten. Without Idella's help, the task of caring for his family must have seemed an almost insurmountable task.

For the first four years of Dick's life, anyone old enough pitched in to help look after Dick. In addition to his older siblings, aunts and uncles on both Merrick's and Idella's side of the family did their part. By the time he was four years old, Merrick's three oldest children, Sylvester, Lloyd and Edith, went to Fairmont to look for work at Owens-Illinois, the glass company, and he was left with no one to help with the farm. So, Merrick quit working the farm and he and Dick moved to Fairmont in 1927. Merrick, Dick, those grown children, including Sylvester and his wife, all lived in the end unit of a four-unit row house there, within walking distance of the factory where they all worked. For some part of the time, young Jimmie was there before he left to join the Marines. Even Opal spent some time with them in Fairmont. It must have been quite an experience, all of them there together, underneath one another's feet. But through it all, Merrick saw to it that Dick started first grade there in 1930.

Perhaps it was the crowded house in Fairmont or perhaps it was a yearning for the farm in Canaan, but before Dick's first year of school ended, Merrick returned home to Canaan. He was stunned by what he found: a rural countryside in the grips of depression. Farm prices had crashed along with the stock market and there was little reason to raise crops and livestock other than to feed one's family. Before long, Merrick, with Dick in tow again, was back to work in Fairmont once more. And once more he soon found his circumstances there more than he cared to endure. Merrick and Dick came home again to the farm in Canaan Valley in 1932. And that is where they stayed.

Dick Moves to the Watchful Care of his Grandmother

When Merrick returned to the Valley, he seemed reenergized to work the farm. Perhaps he had finally emerged from the weight of grief from the loss of Idella, along with the lessening of the responsibilities of tending to growing children. The first summer here, Dick stayed with his grandmother Mary Harr, Idella's mother. Buck and Mary Harr had lived there for many years and Buck had passed away two years earlier at age 78. Now it was only Mary at age 79 and her daughter Bertha, Idella's sister, who remained at home at age 36. When the summer ended, Merrick and Grandma Mary agreed that Dick should stay with her and Dick began the third grade at Harr School, a short walk down the road. And stay he did. For the next eight years, Dick Harr was the ward of his aging grandmother and her spinster daughter, Bertha. He went to school, worked for

Photo of Merrick and Idella Harr children taken in 1925. The four oldest in the rear, left to right are Sylvester, Edith, Hansford (Hank) and James (corncob in mouth); in front, left to right is Mary Opal, Joe, Curtis, and Bertha Harr holding one year-old Richard "Dick" Harr. Photo courtesy of Dick Harr.

Behold! The Land of Canaan

his family, including his father when he needed his help on the farm, and grew into a strong, young man.

Not long after Merrick returned to the Valley, he and others in the family starting building a dance platform on their property along the old county road. Dick remembers the first dance held there on the Fourth of July, 1933. It was not under roof yet, but the floor was finished and it was a beautiful day. The platform often got bad publicity because of drinking and fights. Dick said, "So what! Sometimes there were fights in church!" The platform was an important place where people came to exchange news and for young people to dance. There were not many radios and people needed to come together there on a Saturday evening . There was a "stand" outside the platform for hot dogs and hamburgers and after prohibition ended, beer was sold there. When Dick was about 13 years old, he was allowed to start going to the platform when there was a Saturday night dance. One of Dick's brothers had installed lights for nighttime events using an old 32-volt generator run from an equally old Model T Ford motor. But there was a problem of the motor frequently overheating. Dick recalls he was allowed to get

Harr School

Harr School (in foreground) was located along the old county road through Canaan Valley, today known as Back Hollow Road. Dick Harr says Harr School was so named because so many children from the Harr families attended it. The school was probably built in the 1890s and it is where most of Merrick and Idella's children attended plus, years before, many of Seymour and Lucetta Harr's children and Buck and Mary Harr's younger children years. The school usually had twelve to sixteen students in a given year, all spread across grades one to eight. Note two outhouses far apart from one another behind the school building. Photo courtesy of Dick Harr.

into the platform for free, but it was his job to keep checking the motor's radiator to keep it filled from a nearby rain barrel.

There was no denying that there was moonshine at platform events. That was some of the reason there was a little trouble now and then. Joe Heitz and his friend Albert "Ab" Crossland ran a moonshine still behind where the state park campground is located now and they sold their product to a lot of people in and around the Valley and as far away as Parsons. Dick said that the sale of moonshine put a lot of valuable farm equipment into the fields of Canaan Valley that wouldn't otherwise have been there. And it saved a lot of families from losing their farms and homes when they wouldn't have otherwise been able to pay their taxes.

One time, a still that Joe Heitz and Merrick were operating caught fire and burned down the whole operation. With Merrick Harr helping, Dick says, it was built back even bigger than ever. Merrick's brother Jake sometimes overindulged and after one particularly troublesome dispute between him and his wife Ada sometime around 1922, she finally told the revenuers where the still was located. They came in and dynamited the whole operation and that was the end of moonshining at that location.

Dick remembers the Christmas programs at the Harr School and the other little school houses in the Valley put on each year at that time of the season. The families of all the children would be invited and it was a really big event. Short lengths of logs were cut off and planks laid across them to make benches. The room would be filled with family and friends. But Dick also laments that the programs had very little of the spiritual meaning of Christmas; it was mostly about Santa Claus, with his brother Joe playing the part with great enthusiasm. The children also acted out little comic dialogs they had rehearsed, some in blackface, most of which would be considered offensive to many people today.

Years later when the Harr School closed, the building went back to the ownership of Oscar Heitz who lived there until he died, and then it passed to the Harman Brothers Construction Company, some of whom had married into the Heitz family. They owned it until it was taken by the State of West Virginia for the state park. Dick says that at that time, the state promised to restore the building as a schoolhouse, but, of course, it never made good on that promise.

Dick says living with his grandmother was good and sometimes not so good. It was good that he always had plenty to eat. The not so good was not enough clothing, especially in the wintertime. He recalls one time his father wanted to buy him a new pair of winter boots, made from water repellent rubber, a new product at that time. They did not call them "boots", rather they were known as arctics, but pronounced, *artics*. When his Aunt Berthie heard Merrick intended to buy artics, she shouted, "No! His feet will stink!" So Dick received the old, standard cloth boots; the kind Dick says that usually fell apart from being in the water and it usually happened sometime in January when the snow was deepest. And he added that sometimes he also did not have socks to wear.

One of the summertime pleasures of living in Canaan Valley during this time was great fishing. The Valley was still a well kept secret among anglers outside of this part of West Virginia, and Dick loved to fish. He recalls that Mill Run, a small stream nearby to his grandmother's place had nice brook trout and was an easy walk from home on a sunny afternoon. Today, Mill Run barely has enough water in it to support minnows and the brook trout are long gone.

With all the snow that is visited on Canaan Valley each winter, there was plenty of time to enjoy sledding on the many hills around the Valley. Dick remembers a favorite among the youngsters was to ride on a homemade *Yankee jumper*. It was a long, flat board with a 30-inch vertical post and seat attached. It required great balance and Dick says he was pretty good at navigating it, but there were others who were much better. And it would go really fast if you poured water on the bottom first and let it freeze.

Electricity came to Canaan Valley in the late 1930s. While homes around the Valley were being wired for this new, modern convenience, Bertha was in fear of it and would not permit having it installed in the home place. As long as the house stood in the years ahead, it was always lit with kerosene lamps. During those years when Dick was living there in the 1930s, the evenings could be pretty boring with so little light. Except for those times when they visited others,

Students at Harr School smile for the camera in this picture taken around 1934. The arrow is pointing to Dick Harr. Teacher is Russell Hinkle.
Photo courtesy of Dick Harr.

Behold! The Land of Canaan

bedtime came rather early. Sometimes they would visit a neighbor who had a battery powered radio and they would sit around it and listen to news or music. One time, they went to hear the first Max Schmelling-Joe Lewis heavyweight title fight. Even Grandma Mary went along. Dick remembers that Schmelling won the fight. And he remembers the next time they met, Lewis hammered him in the first round. Dick says Joe Lewis has always been his favorite athlete.

In the 1930s, very few people in Canaan Valley had a car or a truck. But Dick's uncle Brady Harr had an old 1929 Model A Ford and that was a very big deal for him. Brady worked on a road crew during the construction of Route 32, running a jack hammer, and he stayed at the Buck and Mary home along with Dick. Operating a jack hammer was a very dirty, dusty job and he came home every day coated with dirt from head to foot. It was Dick's job to wash Brady's clothes

Of course there was no indoor plumbing and everyone used an outhouse. There was a spring in the hillside behind the house and a pipe was run from there to inside the house for easy access for cooking and washing. There was no shut-off inside the house and the water ran continuously in and down a drain that carried it away. This was particularly important in the wintertime when shutting it off would have quickly caused the pipe to freeze. One time during a very frigid cold spell when everyone was away from home, the pipe froze anyway. Water covered the floor and froze so hard that the door could not be opened. Dick had to open a window to squeeze in and chop the ice from around the door to let the others in. It was a mess.

Quite normally for a young man his age, Dick began to take an interest in some of the young ladies of the community. At age sixteen he had met and enjoyed dancing with one of them at the platform: Mary Jocelyn Raines. Or just Jo. Jo Raines was the daughter of Dow and Carrie Raines Raines and was born and raised in the Flanagan Hill area. Like many of the local families, they enjoyed an evening out at the

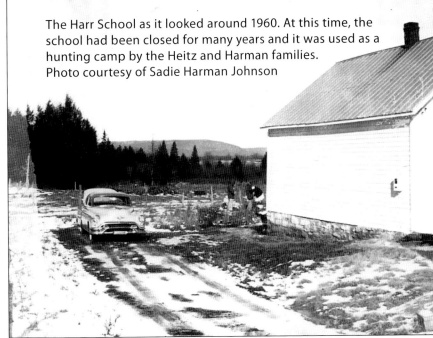

The Harr School as it looked around 1960. At this time, the school had been closed for many years and it was used as a hunting camp by the Heitz and Harman families. Photo courtesy of Sadie Harman Johnson

platform now and then and this is how Dick and Jo became acquainted with one another.

Mary Jocelyn Raines of Flanagan Hill

The Raines family came to the area around Red Creek, also known as Flanagan Hill, in the early 1800s, predating any permanent settlement in Canaan Valley. Carrie Raines was the granddaughter of an early settler, Gabriel Raines. She married Lorenzo Dow Raines, the son of her first cousin, James Raines, and raised a family of nine children, one of which was Jo. Jo Raines had a fairly ordinary childhood, attending Flanagan Hill School and attending local social functions at the platform in her teen years and older. That is where she met her future husband, Dick Harr. Jo contracted polio when she was eleven years old and as a result, had limited use of her right arm for the rest of her life. Contrary to doctor's orders, she refused to keep her arm in a sling and used and exercised it as much as she could, eventually gaining much greater use of it.

Dick Harr Begins Life on his Own

As Dick approached age seventeen and grew closer to Jo Raines, he must have felt the tug of breaking away from life at the home of his grandmother Mary Harr. Dick decided it was time to hit the road. He dropped out of school after the tenth grade at Davis High School. Life

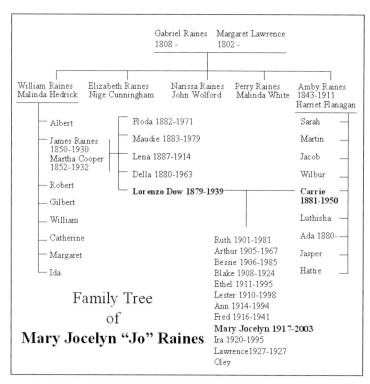

Family Tree
of
Mary Jocelyn "Jo" Raines

Gabriel Raines 1808 - — Margaret Lawrence 1802 -

- William Raines / Malinda Hedrick
  - Albert
  - James Raines 1850-1930 / Martha Cooper 1852-1932
    - Floda 1882-1971
    - Maudie 1883-1979
    - Lena 1887-1914
    - Della 1880-1963
    - **Lorenzo Dow 1879-1939**
  - Robert
  - Gilbert
  - William
  - Catherine
  - Margaret
  - Ida
- Elizabeth Raines / Nige Cunningham
- Narissa Raines / John Wolford
- Perry Raines / Malinda White
- Amby Raines 1843-1911 / Harriet Flanagan
  - Sarah
  - Martin
  - Jacob
  - Wilbur
  - **Carrie 1881-1950**
  - Luthisha
  - Ada 1880-
  - Jasper
  - Hattie

Ruth 1901-1981
Arthur 1905-1967
Bessie 1906-1985
Blake 1908-1924
Ethel 1911-1995
Lester 1910-1998
Ann 1914-1994
Fred 1916-1941
Mary Jocelyn 1917-2003
Ira 1920-1995
Lawrence 1927-1927
Oley

Mary Jocelyn Raines' branch of her family tree goes back to great grandparents born in the early 1800s. Although it is not certain that Gabriel and Margaret Lawrence Raines were born in the Red Creek area, aka Flanagan Hill, it is likely that their five children were, and that was at least two decades before the first permanent settler arrived in Canaan Valley.

with his Grandmother Mary and Aunt Bertha had become somewhat of a drag and he felt beckoned to leave Canaan for a new life of his own. He told Mary and Bertha he was planning to leave but felt a little guilty about it because he did the work they were unable to do such as milking the cows and other farm chores. Dick was able to locate a young man who lived nearby to take over those chores for him which he says opened the way for him to go out on his own. Dick adds that he later learned the new help did not stay very long.

The day came for Dick's departure; he said goodbye to his family where he had lived for the past nine years, caught a ride with a neighbor to Red House, Maryland and there he caught an eastbound Greyhound bus headed for Washington DC. Dick had arranged to room with two other friends from Canaan who had already come to town: Bill Heitz and Willard Johnston. He started looking for a job but soon found that every time he told a prospective employer he was age 17, they said he was too young. Then he applied for a job at an A&P grocery store and when they asked him his age, he said 21. He

The students at Flanagan Hill School pose for a picture in this 1924 photograph. Seven year-old Jo Raines is in the back row (arrow). The teacher, left rear, is Barton Wolford. Photo was taken from the book, *Flanagan Hill History and Memories,* by Grace Hedrick Hamlin Mitchell, with her permission.

Behold! The Land of Canaan

got the job and started stocking shelves and making fifty cents an hour. Dick says the work was hard but it was the best money he had ever made. It was the first supermarket he had ever seen but reflecting on it now, he says it probably was not as large as the *Shop & Save* that is in Davis today. After he was there for a while, he moved to a job as a carpenter's helper at the Pentagon and got a raise to 87 1/2 cents an hour and from there to the site where Andrews Air Force Base was being built. In that job he was a dump truck driver, but he said he had never driven a dump truck before and he did not last very long there. One day, Dick stopped by the draft board in Washington and asked about his draft status. He said he wanted to get married but wanted to know when he might expect to be called. Dick recalls the board member barked at him, "What do you want me to do?!!...tell you a military secret?!" Less than a week later, his notice to report for induction arrived in the mail.

Marriage and Off to War!

The prospect of induction into the Army sent Dick quickly back to Canaan. Arrangements were made and on March 3, 1943, Dick Harr and Jo Raines were married in the home of Pastor Minor Sprague in Oakland, Maryland. He paid him five dollars and he and Jo came back to the Varsity Restaurant in Thomas and had a spaghetti dinner. Concerned that he might lose his job if he didn't get back to DC right away, he took Jo back to the Raines home place in Flanagan Hill and immediately drove back to Washington in his '39 Ford. In a few days, he returned to Canaan and he and Jo came back to DC where he sold his car ("just about gave it away", he says), and they said their goodbye's at the Greyhound station. She boarded a bus for Thomas and he boarded one for Camp Lee, Virginia. Except for a week's furlough that July, they would not see one another again for more than two years. It was also the last time Dick would ever see his father, Merrick.

Dick stayed at Camp Lee only a short time and was soon sent to Fort Leonard Wood, Missouri for basic training. After that, he

was shipped to Shanango, Pennsylvania where troops came in preparation for travel to Europe to join the war in progress there. By late August 1943, Dick found himself in Newport News, Virginia and soon on a Liberty ship headed across the Atlantic with about five hundred other new Army soldiers. After nineteen days at sea, he landed in Casablanca. The war in Africa was over and Dick and others spent their time cleaning and storing weapons, both American and German. Dick says it was "awful work". After moving to another nearby city, he was shipped to Italy where the last of the fighting was going on, even though Italy had already technically surrendered. He spent four months there moving supplies from ships onto the shore, where they were then moved to the fighting. As the battle front moved, so did the location of storing supplies which meant Dick was often changing his location. In June 1944, just as the Allied invasion of France was beginning, Dick moved to Marseilles in southern France and again was busy moving supplies to marshalling areas that moved as the battle front moved. Eventually his work brought him into Germany by the time surrender was finally achieved.

With hostilities winding down in Germany, Dick returned to southern France to await orders. The Army had a system of points awarded to each soldier based on how long

Dick and Jo Harr's first-born was a daughter, Barbara, born while Dick was in Europe during the war. Here Jo holds Barbara in a photo that was probably mailed to Dick and carried by him until he arrived home and could safely tuck it into the family album. Photo courtesy of Dick Harr.

they had been in the service and other factors. Anyone with seventy or more points was eligible for discharge. Dick had sixty-nine points. He received word to prepare to be shipped out for the Pacific to join the war there. But the ship on which he was assigned was delayed for repairs in Gibraltar and while he was waiting there, word came that the bomb had been dropped on Japan and the war was over. The collective sigh of relief from Dick and all those men probably was heard all the way back in Flanagan Hill.

Dick's trip home started with another Atlantic crossing by ship to Newport News, Virginia. Dick recalls seeing movie news of troops returning to New York City with all the fanfare and bands and crowds welcoming them. He said when his ship arrived in Newport News, they were not even greeted by someone playing a harmonica. From there he was sent to Fort Knox, Kentucky where he was discharged from the Army and given a bus ticket home. In late October 1945, Dick carried his duffel bag and walked up the lane to the Raines home place. Jo's mother Carrie was out front and said, "We're

Dow and Carrie Raines around 1930. Photo courtesy of Barbara Harr Alford.

awful glad you're back." Dick said Carrie was a wonderful woman, someone everyone called Granny. Dick walked around back and there was Jo washing clothes and there was Dick's 2 year-old daughter, Barbara, a sweet little girl he was meeting for the first time. It was a day filled with joy and giving thanks for Dick's safe return home. Sadly, the sweetness of the homecoming was dampened by the lingering grief of the loss of Dick's father. Merrick Harr who had come to Canaan Valley by horse and wagon in 1889 had passed away just three months earlier on July 29 and was laid to rest in Cortland Cemetery next to his beloved Idella.

Dick and Jo Harr Finally Begin Their Lives together.

Dick and Jo stayed for a while at Jo's home place in Flanagan Hill but soon they both wanted to get away to a place of their own. Jo's sister Ethel and her husband had recently moved to Parsons from a small farm they rented nearby and Dick and Jo jumped at the chance to move there from the Raines home. The rent was twelve dollars a month. They bought some furniture and a few cows and were soon selling milk on the Carnation Milk Company route. In the summer of 1946, Dick and Jo's second child, a son Lloyd Carl, was born. During this time period, Dick worked on a natural gas pipeline being built through the Valley. By 1948, the estate of Merrick Harr had been settled and Dick and his brother Joe had either bought out Merrick's siblings' interest in the farm or, in some cases, they donated their interest to them. The farm was now the exclusive property of Dick and Joe and their families. Dick and Jo, and Dick's brother Joe, moved onto the farm in spring of 1948 and it became known as the Harr Brothers' Farm.

Dick described the home he and his young family moved into as a "shack". Actually, it was a granary converted to living quarters. It was all they had and they would call it home for the next nine years. Dick and Jo's third baby was born in 1949, a daughter Phyllis. Dick describes these years as times when he and Jo worked very hard to get the farm into shape for cultivation, support a herd of cattle and make time to give

Behold! The Land of Canaan

Young skiers pose for a photo at Cabin Mountain Ski Area, Canaan Valley's first commercial skiing enterprise. From left to right, Dana Parks, Jean Ann Setterstrom, Carl Harr, Jim Arnold, Frank Thompson, Mary Ann Filler, Susan Meyer. Photo courtesy of Dick Harr.

the children the love and attention they needed.

The Harr Brothers' Farm raised beef cattle and grew hay and oats as feed and also grew some wheat and buckwheat. Dick credits the establishment of a stock yard and auction in Terra Alta in the 1940s as one of the important events to bring improvement to the lives of farmers in Canaan Valley. Prior to that time, farmers had to depend on buyers who came to Canaan Valley and often paid so little that it was hardly worth raising the livestock. But farmers had little choice since most had no way to transport their animals to market. When the stockyard opened in Terra Alta, local farmers worked with one another to make vehicles available and selling stock soon became an important source of income to locals.

Another leap forward in the enhancement of lives of farmers in the Valley came in the 1940s when Carnation Milk Company in Oakland began running a milk truck through the Valley to pick up milk from dairy farmers. No longer did farmers need to turn the milk into products like butter, cheese and cottage cheese and sell it to locals themselves. Now they could set out their cans of milk and look for a check in a returned empty milk can every two weeks. It was not much but it was a great help, Dick says.

In the early 1950s, the Ski Club of Washington DC opened a small ski slope on Cabin Mountain on the other side of Route 32 from the farm. The influx of winter visitors over the next few

years brought opportunity for jobs that were badly needed by locals. Dick earned extra money helping move timber and supplies up the mountain by tractor and wagon during the construction phase of the project. Later, he operated the rope tow during the busy weekends when people came by the hundreds to ski in Canaan's beautiful snow. His pay was a dollar an hour. This was Cabin Mountain Ski Area and its success led to the development of Weiss Knob Ski Area just a short distance away in the late 1950s. The Canaan Valley ski industry of today was born of these little skiing start-ups led by people with the vision to see the future of tourism in Canaan Valley. (See "The Heitz Family and the Legacy of Skiing in Canaan Valley", *Chronicles No. 30 & 32*, page 94).

At the same time skiing was making the Valley a tourist destination in the wintertime, Dick was spending the other part of the year as a school bus driver. He started doing that in 1958 at a salary of $125 a month. For the next eighteen years, he drove a Chevy Suburban back to Laneville each morning and carried kids to school in Davis. In those days it was dirt road and was often little more than muddy ruts. But that old Suburban could take on just about any condition that old road was in. Then for the ten years that followed he drove the school bus that ferried the Canaan Valley kids to Davis. He is quick to point out that those twenty-eight years of employment coupled with his time in the

Army has today provided him with a very helpful Social Security check each month.

Dick's brother Joe eventually began working for Union Drilling Co. during the week and came home weekends. Joe's income was used to help build up and support the farm. Dick says Joe "was no farmer" but a great deal is owed to him for all he did to improve the farm.

In 1953, Dick and Jo's son James was born. Daughter Barbara was in the fourth grade at nearby Cosner School and Carl was just starting there as a first grader. Dick and Jo worked with a passion to make ends meet and expand and improve the farm. By this time, they began planning and soon started the construction of their home. It was another task to add to what was already of crush of responsibilities borne by them. But it was completed by 1958, and that was the year they moved into it. Dick says Jo was "in heaven" now that she had a modern kitchen, indoor bathroom, running hot and cold water, a furnace to heat the house and plenty of room for the whole family. For what they had been through, no one deserved it more than the Dick and Jo Harr family.

New Worries Creep into the Happy Life of the Harr Family

The life of the Harr family in their new home might be called idyllic although it was also filled with hard work from daylight to nightfall every day. As Dick neared age forty and with Barbara out of high school and Carl about to graduate, new apprehensions arose among locals in the Valley as rumors began circulating that a new state park might be established there. The rumors had been floating around for several years but were not taken very seriously until a public meeting was held at Blackwater Falls State Park in 1965. Many from the Valley attended to listen to Warden Lane speak about the coming project. When everyone left afterward, most knew it was no longer a rumor.

Letters were sent to all the land owners from which the state would be seeking to purchase land for the park. First, appraisers came that the state had appointed to make an estimate of the value of each property. Dick says that the appraised values the state made were so low that most people hired an independent appraiser. In the case of their 276-acre farm, their hired appraiser arrived at a value $50,000 higher than the state did. It was a clear indication of one of the many underhanded strategies used by the state during the entire process of land acquisition for the park. Nearly every landowner chose to take their condemnation case to court to reach a settlement on the sale price for their property. Again, the state stacked the deck in that process by selecting jury members for each case, most of which were not from Canaan Valley, nor had an understanding of property values there. Dick says the initial offer from the state was $40,000 for the Harr Brothers' Farm but after the court trial, they agreed to accept $80,000. That is $290 an acre for some of the choicest farm land in the Valley. Recalling that the nearby Buck and Mary Harr seventy-six acre home place sold for about $2750 an acre thirty years later, it would not be a stretch that the Harr Brothers' Farm would be a multi-million dollar property today.

Dick and Jo Harr were finally given the deadline of May 31, 1966, to leave their home on the farm. They first moved to a rented home

Mr. Patrick McCaffery
Washington, DC 20002

Dear Patrick,

I appreciate your interest in the recent history of Canaan Valley as pertaining to the development of the State Park. You asked about the attitude of the people whose property was condemned for this purpose. Actually, the large majority of these friends and neighbors are no longer living...so, any thoughts I convey to your on this matter are strictly my own and do not necessarily reflect the opinions of others. I am enclosing these documents pertaining to the farm owned by myself and my brother Joseph. This farm was cleared by my father and his brother during the very early 1900s. It became a very beautiful farm, being level, fertile, and well watered. My brother and I bought the other heirs out when we returned from World War II. The other heirs remain on the legal documents as a result of them retaining their share of mineral rights, but Joe and I owned the surface. Our father died in 1945, just a few months before we were discharged.

Rumors were circulating perhaps as early as 1963 or 64 that the state was going to establish a park in the valley. For a year or two these reports were not taken very seriously. However, a meeting at Blackwater Lodge perhaps, in 64 and attended by Warden Lane, the director of the WV dept of natural resources where it appeared in no uncertain terms that the state was really going to move forward on this project.

Not long afterward the DNR sent appraisers around to the various homesteads for the purpose of setting a "Fair Market Value" on each place. This began to initiate considerable anxiety among the landowners, since the said appraisers did not seem to take their work too seriously. It began to appear that these men were only interested in setting a value on property only to answer the desires of the state, resulting in the landowners having to hire their own appraisers to somewhat counter the state appraisers. Generally resulting in considerably high figures, so the alternative was to go to court, which generally resulted in a higher figure. In our own case we gained from $40,000 to $80,000 but we had to pay our lawyer $10,000 to handle the case.

Upon being evicted, several of the residents moved from the valley. Some did not realize enough pay for their homes to reestablish in a like manner in other areas. Each case being tried separately caused a variance in what each jury considered a fair award. Each trial had a separate jury. This variance was not conducive to the best attitudes among the people themselves. Some seemed to fare better in court than others. This may have been the result of some lawyers doing a better job for their clients. Much to my disgust, our own prosecuting attorney chose to represent the DNR against the residents, who had elected him to office several times. Needless to say, he was not successful in subsequent elections.

Some of the evicted families moved to other counties, while some bought parcels of land here in the valley. A few had other land in the valley besides what the DNR took. As for me and my brother, we purchased home sites in the valley. We received about $250.00 per acre for some of the very best land but had to pay $1,000.00 an acre of unapproved land covered with brush and thorns, making it more expensive to build on.

Inflation has grown by leaps and bounds since then, about 1966. I understand that today a desirable acre of land, if one is available, will run $10,000.00 Five acre lots on Timberland Development run about $30,000.00. It is quite obvious that the cost of property in this valley rests squarely on the backs of landowners who were evicted. Those who lived outside the park zone have had the opportunity to more or less "cash in" on a golden opportunity to make good sales. I don't believe there is any hard feelings present against these landowners. We do not blame them for taking advantage of a good opportunity.

Many homes have been built in the valley during the past several years. These homes are quite expensive and have added a great deal to the tax base of Tucker County. Some of the families who have moved to the area have become involved in community affairs and have become a real asset to the community. We certainly need and appreciate them. Many of the homes though are simply second homes, being available for rent or just weekend or vacation homes.

Many businesses have developed, giving employment to a great number of people. However, I believe we have not been without our share of the "fast buck" characters who might remind us of the old south carpet bagger.

Canaan Valley Landowners Assn. was developed a few years ago. One accomplishment was a set of zoning laws for the valley. This may have caused a few disputes between old settlers and new homeowners, but I believe it has been all for the good of all concerned.

Other controversial matters arise from time to time, but thanks to some level headed volunteer servants in the community, things continue to develop in the pursuit of progress. In spite of the ups and downs in the past we here in the valley will continue to be optimistic, for where could one find another place so blessed with beauty and inhabited with such lovely people. We are too busy counting our blessings to be bothered with ill feelings toward one another.

Patrick, I don't know if this is what you had in mind or not. But this pretty well sums up my feelings, that I think are pretty much the feelings of my good neighbors. If you can use this in any way, I would appreciate what you come up with.

     Sincerely,

     Richard Harr

P.S. One more thing concerning the mineral rights that the DNR took along with the land, because one would not be allowed to drill on a state park. However, the DNR proceeded to have an offset well drilled slanting the drilling tools in under the park enabling them to bleed off the gas that I think rightfully belong to the evicted landowner. This, I do very much resent.

This is a transcription of a letter written by Dick Harr in 1992 to a newspaper reporter who was seeking information for an article about the establishment of Canaan Valley State Park. The reader is left to decide what was in Dick Harr's mind and heart when he wrote it and what measure of person he is based on his words. Letter provided courtesy of Dick Harr.

1967 snapshot of Dick and Jo Harr taken on the day their daughter Phyllis was married. Photo courtesy of Dick Harr.

nearby where they lived for the next year while a new home was built on a lot along Cortland (now Sagebrush) Lane, across from where the Deerfield condominium development is located today. Dick, Jo and children Phyllis and Jimmie moved into that new home on December 23, 1967. At that time, daughter Barbara was working in Baltimore and son Carl was serving in Vietnam.

Dick's brother Joe moved into a cabin in Stringtown in May of 1966, a few miles south of the Valley. He became a local water well driller, using his own well drilling equipment. He married Ruby Ware from Buckhannon and they moved into a home on Cortland Road in the Valley. He lived there until his death in 1988.

In the irony of this event in Dick's life, he was later hired as a carpenter by the state park to make some improvements in the structure of his former house, now used as a residence by the park. He says he learned through the grapevine it was used by the superintendent for a weekly poker game for him and some of his cronies.

For all that has befallen Dick and his family at the hands of the state of West Virginia in the loss of their home and farm in the Valley, he harbors very little bitterness today about that episode in his life. He feels it happened, it is done and over, and there is no merit in wallowing in anger and self-pity over it. To know Dick is to understand that he really does feel that way.

The Life of the Harr Family After Leaving the Farm

In the years that followed, all four of Dick and Jo's children married and moved away from Canaan, had families and lived their lives elsewhere. Jo passed away peacefully in 2003 at age 86 and was laid to rest in Cortland Cemetery. Daughter Barbara is now retired and lives with her husband Jim Alford near Leadmine in Tucker County. Carl is retired and lives with his wife Maria Partosa in a home just a few minutes walk from Dick's home. Phyllis is retired and lives in the Washington, DC area. Jimmie lives and works in Florida and is married to Marylyn Hostetler. Dick has many grandchildren and a growing number of great grandchildren.

Today, Dick Harr busies himself with many

A photo of the home place on the Harr Brothers' Farm around the time the legal proceedings were underway by the state of West Virginia to acquire it for the new Canaan Valley State Park. Route 32 runs left to right just beyond the home and outbuildings and the hillside beyond is the site of Cabin Mountain Ski Area which began operation there in the early 1950s. Photo courtesy of Dick Harr.

Behold! The Land of Canaan

activities throughout the year. He is a lay leader and Sunday School teacher at Buena Chapel in the Valley. He also plays the piano during the worship service, a skill he taught himself as a young man. The winters are the most difficult for him to pass the time because he cannot get out of the house and can no longer drive a car due to his failing eyesight. Carl gets him out to wherever he needs to go, and he looks forward to his monthly visit to the barber with his old friend Glenn Miller who lives nearby. In the warm months of the year, Dick keeps his yard looking neat and trim, plants and cares for a garden behind his home, works with Carl in caring for Cortland Cemetery and acts as the master of ceremony at the monthly seniors' lunch at the Flanagan Hill Community Center. He loves to chat with visitors, particularly to talk about his life in Canaan Valley and all he remembers that has happened here. He tells his stories with dash and snap and usually ends it with a gusto-filled laugh. For all he has been

though, his passion for life seems as strong as ever, charged with a love of Canaan Valley and its people and lives his life filled with pride of his roots deep in West Virginia.

Photos of Dick Harr leading activities at the monthly seniors' lunch at Flanagan Hill Community Center. Dick opens the program with the playing and singing of "Happy Birthday" to all those celebrating a birthday that month. Above he jokes with Josephine Gruden in front of him and Kate Hedrick to the right.

Frances Tekavec passed peacefully away at home on September 8, 2008. Born July 25, 1914, in a lumber camp in Dry Fork, Fannie, as she was fondly known to everyone, married Frank Tekavec in 1934 and was the mother of five children. She had a keen memory of the early years around Davis and Canaan Valley and consented to an oral history session with TCHHEP members in the home of her daughter Veronica Staron in 2005. Her stories of the Tekavec family in Davis and in the lumber camps were part of the inspiration for Cindy Phillips' fictional tale of history, "The Lone Survivor of Camp 72", Chronicles No. 16, that appeared in *Behold! The Land of Canaan* 2009. We are very thankful to have known Fannie and for her kind contribution to our historical knowledge of the Tucker County Highlands. Photo courtesy of Fannie's daughter, Veronica (Tekavec) Staron.

TWO FRIENDS
Bid Us Farewell

Canaan Valley resident Dorothy Thompson passed away October 1, 2008. She was born August 5, 1920, near Masontown, Pennsylvania where her father was a coal miner. During the Great Depression she had an opportunity to learn weaving as part of Roosevelt's New Deal educational programs. At the start of WWII, she met and married Ben Thompson and spent the rest of her life in Canaan Valley raising a family, helping manage the Thompson farm and teaching weaving. Ben's Old Loom Barn, where she worked and taught weaving for more than a quarter-century is a Canaan Valley landmark. Dorothy graciously spent many oral history interview hours talking about her long and interesting life in Canaan Valley. To have known Dorothy has been a blessing to those of us in Tucker County Highlands History and Education Project (TCHHEP), and she will be greatly missed.
Photo courtesy of Dorothy's daughter, Sarah (Thompson) Fletcher.

Places

Fire Tower, Canaan Mtn., near Davis, W.VA.

Altora 350

Canaan Valley—
Massive
Mountain
—Weathered Away

Canaan is often cited as 'A Bit of Canada Gone Astray,' but a more accurate description might be, 'A Massive Mountain Weathered Away.' The region we call Canaan Valley today was once part of a collection of mountains that would rival, if not surpass, today's Himalayas. It's an amazing story how this patch of ground evolved from what it was early in Earth's history to what it is today, and how it influenced the lives of those who first settled here, then those who came later and finally those of us who live here today.

If we turn back the clock 250 million years we'd find the region we call Canaan Valley located just north of the Equator, positioned in an east-west direction, and hidden under a massive mountain range. How it got there and how it got to where it is today makes for an interesting tale.

The world we know with its seven continents is much different from the world of long ago. Forces deep within our Earth power the movement of a set of tectonic plates that comprise the surface of our world. These plates persistently move, bump into and grind against each other and in doing so, the surface structure of our world is continuously transformed.

Above, an awesome view of Canaan Valley, the remains of a massive mountain weathered away. Photo by the late Elliott Ours, provided courtesy of Margot Ours.

As tectonic plates collide, they compress the Earth's crust caught between them, bending and folding it into mountain ranges. Over one billion years ago the continent that would one day become North America collided with other continents to form a large supercontinent called Rodinia. As this collision took place, the sediment, which had been on the ocean floor that separated these continents, was caught in the collision and thrust up onto the side of the primitive North American continent, forming a Himalayas-sized mountain range geologists refer to as the Grenville Mountains.

During that time the geography of the Earth looked nothing like it does today. The region that would become North America was experiencing a warm climate because it was positioned near the Equator, with today's east coast facing south. Over the next few hundred million years the continents drifted apart again and the Grenville Mountains eroded, depositing sediment into vast oceans that existed on both sides of the mountain range. The rocks that formed the core of the Grenville Mountains make up the very deepest layer of rock beneath our Appalachians.

Starting about 470 million years ago the continental plates began to come together again. This time the initial convergence of the plates spawned extensive volcanic activity forming islands along what would become the eastern coast of North America and eventually forming a mountain range called the Taconics. The forces induced by this collision caused the crust in our region to sink, forming a broad shallow inland sea known as the Appalachian Basin. This sea teamed with microscopic marine life that, as it died, deposited its calcium-rich bodies on the basin floor. As the Taconic Mountains eroded, the basin filled with sediment covering the layers of marine organisms and contributing to the their eventual transformation into limestone. This limestone would one day be quarried in Canaan Valley, crushed for the base layers of its roads and ground into dust for sweetening its fields of grass and hay.

This basin area also became rich in vegetation. As the region was still located along the Equator, the vegetation growth was lush and abundant. Ocean levels repeatedly rose and fell covering deposits of vegetation with sediment from the eroding Taconics. Under pressure and with time, these layers of vegetation were transformed into deposits of coal. This is the coal that would make the town of Thomas in its early years one of the most famous coal towns in America, bringing the railroad and steam locomotive to haul it away to fuel the fires of the country's industrial revolution a century ago.

The continents continued to drift and move and about 380 million years ago Europe collided with

the northeast part of North America forming the Acadian Mountains. At the same time, the continent of Africa collided with North America forming the supercontinent Pangea. At the heart of this supercontinent the Earth's crust was folded and compressed to form a massive mountain range we know today as the Appalachians. At the peak of their formation, 250 million years ago, the Appalachians were probably every bit as high as the Himalayas.

From that time to the present, the continents drifted apart with North America moving slowly northward and taking on its more familiar north-south orientation. The once massive Appalachians have eroded, creating the mountain range familiar to us today.

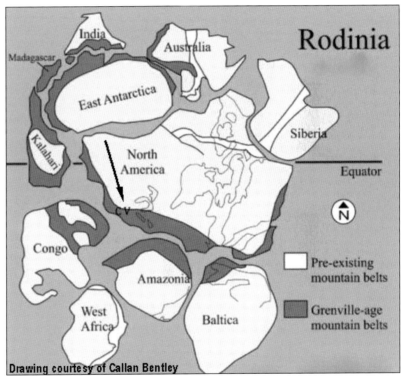

Drawing courtesy of Callan Bentley

About 700 million years ago, the earth's tectonic plates clustered together to make up the super-continent of *Rodinia* (upper right). Approximate location of Canaan Valley denoted by CV (at arrow). Driven by currents in the molten interior of the earth, those plates have slowly moved from that orientation to the positions they hold today. The world's mountains are the result of these plates bumping into one another through the ages.

The supercontinent of Pangea (lower right) as it appeared 250 million years ago. The massive Appalachian Mountains sit astride the equator. The approximate location of Canaan Valley is denoted by **CV** (arrow). (Drawing courtesy of the University of California Museum of Paleontology).

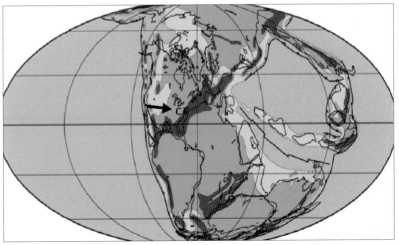

Canaan Valley History—
UNCOVERED

An abandoned quarry today at the intersection of Route 32 and Back Hollow Road in the south end of Canaan Valley. Limestone found here was removed, crushed and used for road bed material when this highway was built in the 1930s. In years past when the Valley was mainly agricultural, farmers who found a limestone outcrop on their land would crush and pulverize it for use on their fields. Now mostly grown over, a number of these small limestone-digs can still be found, some with rusted-out crushers standing nearby.

Canaan Valley is comprised largely of limestone formed out the deposited marine organisms that sank to the floor of the Appalachian Basin some 350 million years ago. The sediment that covered these marine deposits from the eroding Taconic Mountains has itself been transformed into siltstone and sandstone. As the Earth's crust was crushed and folded during the time the Appalachians were being formed, some regions bulged upward (geologists call these areas anticlines) while other regions folded downward (termed synclines). The region that comprises Canaan Valley is made up of layers of sedimentation that have been bulged up. Running down the center of the Valley is a feature known as the Blackwater Anticline. The rock layers that underlie the Valley dip downward from this centerline.

At some point as erosion took place, the sandstone cap layer which formerly existed some 2,000 feet above today's valley floor was breached, exposing the underlying siltstone and limestone layers. Limestone and siltstone are more susceptible to erosion by water and over time, layers of these materials have been washed away. The sandstone layer that formed a cap over the Valley (known as Pottsville sandstone) can still be found along today's ridge tops of Canaan and Cabin Mountains. This same wear-resistant sandstone layer also forms the top ledge of Blackwater Falls.

Lying above this sandstone layer were most certainly layers of coal formed out of the deposited vegetation from over 300 million years ago. This coal, as well as the multiple layers of sedimentation that existed above it, eroded away long ago. The seams of coal found to the north and west of the Valley, and which underlie Dolly Sods to the east, are part of these same deposits.

Humans have existed in this region of North America for 10,000 years, a mere heartbeat in geologic time. Geology has always played an important role in shaping human history, and the human history of Canaan Valley is no exception. There is evidence that while ancient people inhabited nearby low-lying areas such as Horseshoe Bend as long ago as 10,000 years, there is little evidence of any such settlements within Canaan Valley. We also know that as Europeans arrived on the east coast and moved westward they largely avoided the Canaan Valley area. There are good reasons why Canaan Valley was settled only 150 years ago and the fundamental reason can be traced to its geology.

As the sandstone layer was breached and the valley we know today was created, it developed into what geologists term a frost hollow. Ringed by ridges that surround it, cold air settles into the valley and is trapped, contributing to a climate typically found much further north. Its elevation and geographical location played a critical role. Continental drift over the past 250 million years has moved its location from near the Equator to almost halfway towards the North Pole. This same drift also rotated the orientation of the Valley from an east-west one to largely a north-south one, placing it on the windward side of the Appalachian Mountains where it captures moisture-laden air driven east by the prevailing winds and resulting in substantial snowfalls in winter and rains during summer. The massive virgin spruce, hemlock, and black cherry forests and the impassable rhododendron thickets found by the early visitors and settlers were a direct result of these geological and geographical features. It is these features that made Canaan Valley an uncomfortable and foreboding place for human habitation and the reason it was avoided for so long.

When early settlers finally did choose to settle in the Valley, where they located can also be attributed to the local geology. Naturally, they chose locations on the drier flat ground within the valley where water was readily available. Many valley locations have excellent free-flowing springs where water collected along the ridges emerges through cracks and fissures in the limestone that makes up the valley floor. The limestone itself also served as foundation stones and building blocks for their dwellings. The inaccessibility of the Valley certainly contributed to the fact that, while it possessed one the greatest virgin spruce forests in the east, it was one of the last areas timbered in the region.

The same geological features that kept Canaan Valley isolated for so long contribute to its uniqueness today. Its cold snowy winters and cool pleasant summers make it an ideal location for today's vacationers. While its isolation has been breached by modern-day communications technology and transportation systems, the fundamental geological features are still here to be appreciated.

Take time to stand on one of the ridge tops above the Valley, but rather than looking down, look up and try to imagine the mountain peak that once stood perhaps 20,000 feet above the valley floor. Bend over and pick up a small piece of sandstone that caps these ridges and

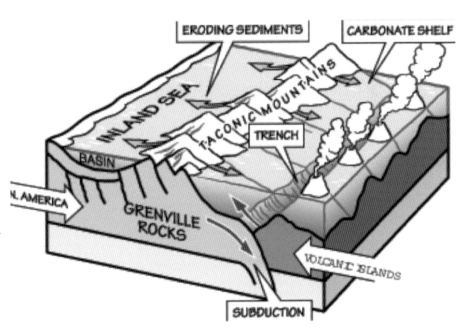

About 470 million years ago, the Taconic Mountains formed along the east cost of North America. A shallow inland sea, the Appalachian Basin, existed behind these mountains and contained the region that became Canaan Valley. (Diagram courtesy of Picconi, J. E. 2003. The Teacher-Friendly Guide to the Geology of the Southeastern U.S. Paleontological Research Institution, Ithaca, NY.)

appreciate that it was once part of a pre-Appalachian mountain range formed some 470 million years ago only to be eroded and deposited into a vast prehistoric inland sea before being thrust up to become part of the great Appalachians.

Later, sit on a block of limestone rock that makes up the valley floor and consider the journey it has been on. Three hundred fifty million years ago it was a small bit of marine life swimming in a warm inland sea before it too became part of the underlying structure of the Appalachians. And be thankful to be in this place at this time because in the not too distant future, at least respective to geologic time, all of this will be washed away to await its next great adventure and transformation.

Blackwater Falls is a benefactor of this same sandstone which lies atop much softer stone beneath it, forming one of West Virginia's most famous landmarks. This old photo plainly shows the tough caprock that forms the falls (and the two men sitting on the edge of the precipice).

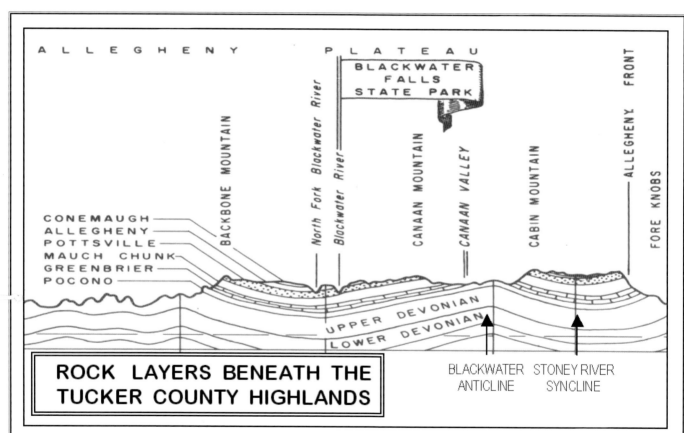

ROCK LAYERS BENEATH THE TUCKER COUNTY HIGHLANDS

This diagram is a geologist's view of the layers of rock beneath the highlands surrounding Canaan Valley. The various rock layers were assigned names (listed on the left) many years ago as geologists first identified them and developed theories about their origin. The *Pottsville* that lies atop Canaan and Cabin Mountains is a very hard sandstone that is resistant to erosion. The *Greenbrier* beneath it is an easily eroded limestone that outcrops across wide areas of Canaan Valley. The nature of these beds of rock are responsible for the landscape of Canaan Valley and mountains surrounding them that we see today. Diagram adapted from a graphic courtesy of the West Virginia Geological and Economic Survey.

Behold! The Land of Canaan

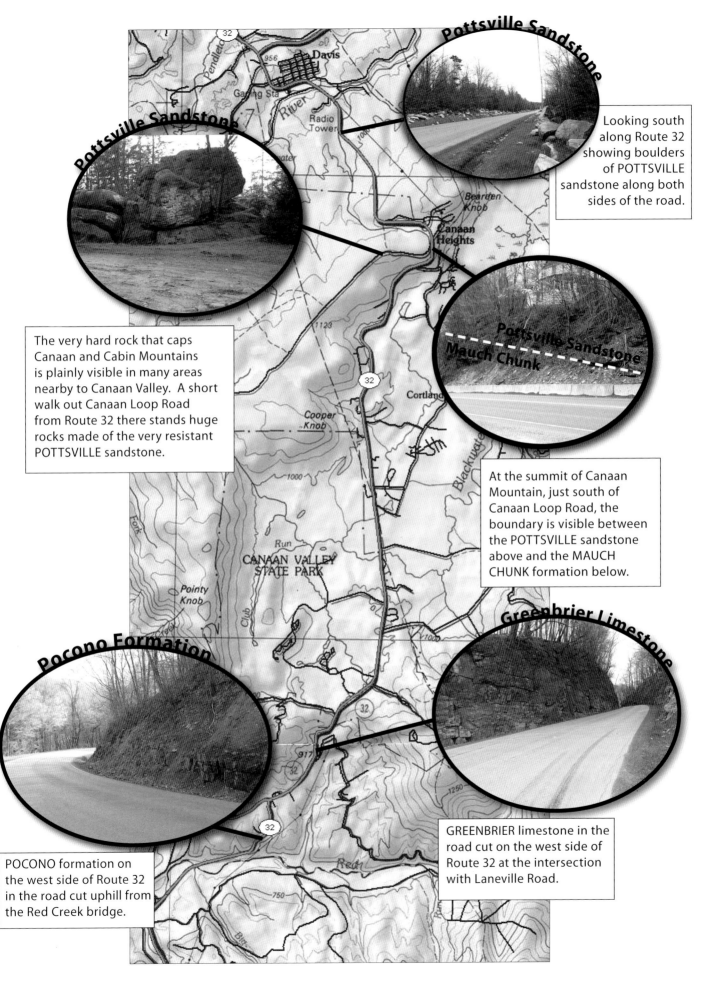

Pottsville Sandstone

Pottsville Sandstone

Looking south along Route 32 showing boulders of POTTSVILLE sandstone along both sides of the road.

The very hard rock that caps Canaan and Cabin Mountains is plainly visible in many areas nearby to Canaan Valley. A short walk out Canaan Loop Road from Route 32 there stands huge rocks made of the very resistant POTTSVILLE sandstone.

Pottsville Sandstone
Mauch Chunk

At the summit of Canaan Mountain, just south of Canaan Loop Road, the boundary is visible between the POTTSVILLE sandstone above and the MAUCH CHUNK formation below.

Greenbrier Limestone

Pocono Formation

POCONO formation on the west side of Route 32 in the road cut uphill from the Red Creek bridge.

GREENBRIER limestone in the road cut on the west side of Route 32 at the intersection with Laneville Road.

My Childhood Memories of Canaan Heights

After many years of going to the end of the road at Camp 70 to get permission from Mr. Love at his home there to go through his farm to the "pocket" during deer season, three men and some friends decided not to battle the Canaan Valley weather any more. In 1946, my father Harlan Gill, grandfather Ed Calebaugh and uncle Fred Calebaugh decided to search for a place to buy some land to erect a hunting cabin. My father was very familiar with the area because his father, Ralph Gill, had taken Harlan to the Davis, Thomas and Canaan area many times as a young man.

While Harlan and my mother Frances Calebaugh Gill were looking for real estate, they

This photo of Janice Gill Hardman's parents Harlan and Frances Calebaugh Gill was taken in honor of their 50th wedding anniversary. Photo courtesy of Janice Gill Hardman.

met Naomi Mosser and her husband Glendie in Canaan Heights. They purchased a building lot in Canaan Heights from the Mossers and, along with my grandfather and uncle, built a large one-room cabin on the lot. I am Janice, the only daughter of Harlan and Frances, and I was eleven years old in 1946.

Money was scarce at the time, but my grandfather Calebaugh owned quite a lot of property in Sistersville, West Virginia. They tore down an old house there, saved the nails, and hired a man with a flat bed truck to bring everything to Canaan. After the cabin was built, but before it was finished, my dad and mom and I came as a family and began working on the finishing touches. The cabin was located along the old Davis Road, now called Canaan Heights Road.

In the summertime, several families in Canaan Heights would get together on the weekends. Pete Milkint, a polio survivor, built the stone house across the highway and he was always having parties and inviting everyone. Later he married and moved to Silver Lake where they built the smallest church in West Virginia–where it still stands. Today, Sam and Amy Goughnour are the owners of the Milkint home in Canaan Heights.

The Heights became like a small community. The Mossers had six grandchildren, the Wolfes had two children, and I was always together with them having a great time. We are still close friends after all these years. Other families who participated in life in the Heights were Phelps (the Mosser's grandchildren), Young, Jones, Wiblin and Richardson.

One of the things we enjoyed was when my father took us to visit the Graham farm on Freeland Road. They had pet trout. I could put my hand in the water and they would swim over and lay on it.

Janice Gill's grandfather Ed Calebaugh (left) and her uncle Fred Calebaugh posing with trophy deer around 1950 at the Gill cabin in Canaan Heights. Photo courtesy of Janice Gill Hardman.

One evening Mrs. Mosser (we called her Bobbo) came down to visit at the cabin. She asked my father if he would like to buy the lot next to our cabin. The lot bordered the National Forest and he knew there was a nice spring on it, and so he and my mother bought it. On the day Bobbo offered the lot to Harlan, he had only twenty dollars with him, so Bobbo took that as a down payment and wrote a receipt for it on the wall of the cabin.

I loved the Mossers; they were like another set of grandparents. For a time, Glendie worked part time as a fire warden at the Bearden Knob fire tower—and I often delivered lunch to him while he was on duty. His favorite meal was a sandwich made on homemade bread baked by my mother. Visiting the tower was a thrill for a twelve–year–old girl. Unfortunately, in 1951 we were all grief-struck when Glendie Mosser was killed in an automobile accident while driving down the mountain to Parsons. Bobbo later gave me the lot behind our cabin.

My grandparents Ed and Olie Calebaugh, my uncle Fred and aunt Opal, and my family and I came to Canaan often. During the years, deer hunting became quite an occasion. My grandfather did all the cooking and everyone was always welcome at mealtime.

My father has told the story about him killing a large buck in Weimer Hollow, below us on the Davis side of Canaan Mountain, and dragging it up the mountain

Janice Gill Hardman's sons Robert and Fred show off their day's catch of fish at the Gill cabin in Canaan Heights about 1970. Janice's father Harlan Gill imbued in her and her sons a love of the outdoors and instilled in them an understanding of the need for conservation of the beautiful world around them. Photo courtesy of Janice Gill Hardman.

The Gill family cabin in Canaan Heights in the 1960s, after a front porch had been added to the original structure. The cabin is gone today but that place along the old Davis Road holds many wonderful memories for the Gill family. Photo courtesy of Janice Gill Hardman.

A 1930s photo of Glendie and Naomi Mosser who were close friends of the Gill family in Canaan Heights when they built their cabin there in the 1940s. Photo courtesy of Bill Phelps, grandson of the Mossers.

back to the cabin. When he arrived at the top of the hill he was exhausted; some men traveling the old Davis Road saw him and came to the rescue. During those years, the trees were still so small that it was no problem to see him from the road. This was the late 1940s. Of course, now the forest has all grown back on the mountain. About this same time, I used to walk to the old fire tower on Canaan Loop Road. I would sit on the huge rocks around the tower until one day I heard a bear coming my way, and I very rapidly

came back down the road. I think the tower was torn down shortly thereafter.

My father loved to be outdoors and was exploring all the time. He bought an old Jeep. Friends, family and grandchildren learned about the Canaan area, including my sons Robert and Fred who learned a love of the outdoors from their many visits to Canaan. Harlan and my mother never knew a stranger, and they made many friends. Like her father Ed, her kitchen was open to everyone.

Rooms were added to the cabin later on. After my parents retired, they lived there from April to November each year and then returned to their Clarksburg home for the winter.

Around the early 1960s a forest ranger cabin was built on the old Davis Road. It did not seem to be there for very long, but behind it were several trees and pines planted in a small meadow. Above and to the left of where the cabin stood is a large spring that was piped down to the road. People used to stop and get good, cold water there. You have to watch for it as you walk or drive by or you will miss it. The grass and weeds have almost camouflaged it. It is known as *the government spring* because it comes out of the ground on National Forest land.

My father, Harlan Gill, passed away at age 93 and my mother, Frances, at 87, but their wonderful memories and teachings will always live on in my heart.

A section from the 1960 edition of the State Road Commission of West Virginia highway map of Tucker County showing Canaan Heights along Route 32, south of Davis. Although this is the earliest map that can be found showing it as a named community, 93-year old Canaan Valley resident, Ruth Cooper Allman, recalls that it was known to locals as *Canaan Heights* as early as the 1930s. Copy of the original map provided courtesy of Sharon Parsons Stavrakis.

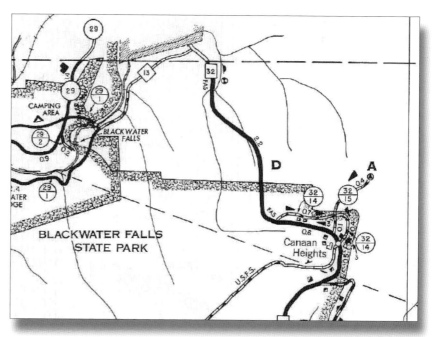

Behold! The Land of Canaan

THEN & *now*

Canaan Tower 1930s

Altovrn 3500

Fire Tower, Canaan Mtn., near Davis, W.VA.

The Fire Towers at Canaan Heights

Canaan Lookout Fire Tower was built around 1920 and was one of the first fire towers established following the creation of the Monongahela National Forest. The stark lack of trees along Canaan Loop Road on Canaan Mountain at that time made it suitable for the lookout shelter to be perched on the high rocks rather than with the long legs common to most fire towers. With the new growth of trees in the 1930s and 1940s that gradually obscured the view, the lookout lost its usefulness and was replaced by a new fire tower on nearby Bearden Knob.

Canaan Tower Location 2008

Bearden Knob Fire Tower was used by the Forest Service in the years following the decommissioning of the Canaan Lookout fire tower. This tower is also gone today, replaced by an automated weather and air pollution sampling station. This facility includes a web camera atop the tall mast that looks across Canaan Valley toward Dolly Sods. This wonderful view of the Valley can be seen during daylight hours at: *http://www.fsvisimages.com/doso1/doso1.html*.

Bearden Tower circa 1955

Bearden Tower circa 2008

Passages of Lives of the Church and Town's are Closely Linked: St. John's Lutheran Church Shares History with Davis

1898 Fowler map of Davis with inset enlargement of St. John's Lutheran Church which stands out as one of the largest buildings in town. In just thirteen years, the town had undergone a dramatic conversion from a stump-filled clearing in the woods to a prosperous town of humming business and industry with an orderly network of streets, neat rows of homes and churches of four different denominations.

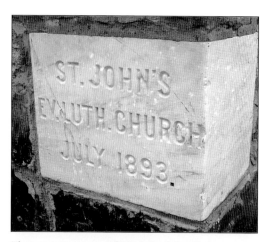

The cornerstone of St. John's Lutheran Church today.

This is a story of the creation and life of a new church in a new town, both built before the start of the twentieth century with the optimism of a prosperous time. The story begins with the development of a railroad, a town and then a church. St. John's Lutheran, a large dark green structure at the corner of Blackwater Avenue and Third Street was the fourth church built in the new town of Davis, West Virginia. It has been in continuous operation since those days and the building has not been greatly altered. Both the town and the church have thrived and struggled in the boom and bust times that followed.

United States Senator (1873-1883) Henry Gassaway Davis and his brothers Thomas and William had heard about the inhospitable wilderness of impassable laurel brakes and thick forests around the Blackwater River, but they envisioned an opportunity for development. They began purchasing land with the intention of developing a railroad and a town to be the center of a lumber and coal business. Between 1871 and 1873, the Davis brothers purchased 23,000 acres of land, and between 1880 and 1883 they purchased another 34,000 acres.

The West Virginia Central and Pittsburg Railroad was chartered in 1881 with Henry Gassaway Davis as President. The railroad construction began at Piedmont, West Virginia in April 1880 and arrived at the new town of Davis on November 1, 1884. The railroad continued to Parsons in 1888, Elkins in 1889, and Durbin in 1903, connecting to

Behold! The Land of Canaan

other lines from Durbin to Charleston in 1905 and completing the link through the mountains between the Baltimore & Ohio and the Chesapeake & Ohio Railroads. The entire company interests were sold in 1905 for $19 million.

While the railroad was being built, Senator Davis had hired Robert Ward Eastham, who had been farming in Canaan Valley since 1876, to clear land for the town of Davis (See "Robert Eastham, A Transplanted Virginian", p. 18). The town was often called "Stump Town" because a person could walk on the stumps from one side of town to the other without touching the ground. James Parsons was hired to lay out the town. Regular train service began in 1885. The first lumber mill, Rumbarger's, opened in 1886, but lumber was being cut earlier in anticipation of the mill's opening.

By November of 1889, there were 909 persons counted in a census in the soon to be chartered town of Davis. The Davis City Times of May 1, 1891 stated, "Upon the spot where six years ago there was nothing but a forest, through which roamed at will the deer, bear and other animals, there now stands a live business town having a population of 1500 people, and where two large sawmills, a box factory, shingle mill, large tannery, mine and railroad with their rush and roar, give to our town the appearance already of what it will be in the near future. The prospects for Davis were never brighter than

they are now. We are glad that this is so." By 1895 the population was close to 3,000. Davis was booming.

As businesses opened, people realized a different need–a spiritual one. In 1953 Felix Robinson wrote, "The reason why so many of our communities have become ghost towns has been their neglect of the spiritual life. Before Rumbarger's band saw-mill was whining in the Great Wilderness (what the Davis area had previously been called) the people were singing the songs of Zion." In 1884 Presbyterian services began in a box car. The Northern Methodists and Presbyterians completed their church buildings in 1886-87 on opposite corners at Fourth Street and Thomas Avenue; the Free Methodist Church was completed in 1893 on the corner of Fairfax Avenue and Third Street. The first church was built before the first school or hospital; going to "meetinghouse" (church and Sunday School) was a regular part of life. The next church to be built was St. John's Lutheran. It was erected by the Greider brothers with the same hopeful vision as the town with seating for over four hundred people. The church was chartered on February 23, 1893 with thirty-two members. Planning for the church had begun in 1892 with the work of Gettysburg Seminary student J. F. W. Kitzmeyer who, upon graduation, was called as the first pastor.

Pastor Kitzmeyer conducted catechetical class after 4:00 P.M. two or three evenings each week

1885 photo of Davis. Photo courtesy of Ruth Cooper Allman.

The massive bell that was installed when St. John's was built in 1894 still hangs in the tower that adjoins the church. The bell had rarely been rung in recent years due to uncertainty about the condition of the framework on which it hung. Pastor Allen Schwarz did ring the bell in 2002 on the one year anniversary of the September 11, 2001 attack on the World Trade Center. Recent restoration work on the church included strengthening the bell tower and once again the bell can be heard on Sunday mornings as it calls the faithful to worship. Photo courtesy of Friends of the 500th.

for any child that wanted to come (and many did). He held children spellbound for an hour and a half, and after the lesson he told a Bible story and one of Anderson's or Grimm's fairy tales. Church met on Sundays and midweek, but the midweek services were discontinued in 1895. St. John's building is a massive structure: eighty-three feet long by fifty-two feet wide with an eighty foot bell tower and a distance of forty-six feet from floor to vaulted ceiling. The

cornerstone was laid July 30, 1893, but a fire that damaged the Blackwater Lumber Company delayed completion. The building, including the forty to fifty-foot long exposed A-Frame roof trusses, was made from local virgin spruce timbers joined together with wooden dowels. The lumber for the trusses was cut at the Beaver Creek Lumber Company in Davis and was installed under the supervision of an experienced shipbuilder. The exterior was covered with dark green wooden German lap siding (described in print of the day as shingles). A large stained glass window of Martin Luther was installed in the front of the church with stained glass images of the four evangelists and others on the sides with a portrayal of Christ over the altar.

The church was heated with two coal and wood burning furnaces in excavated areas beneath the floor. In Paul Poerschke's 1990 history of the church he wrote, "Heating of the massive structure in the severe winters on the mountaintop has been a perennial problem to the present day. Vivid memories of frost on the walls of the church, members of the congregation and pastor worshipping in overcoats and freezing to the seats, still prevail." In 1914 heating was changed to natural gas radiators along the walls. Light was, at first, provided by kerosene lamps, then by gas lights with mantles and later with electricity (Davis had several homes and the town's streetlights run by electricity as early as 1893). Tuning wires were installed at the base of

The Sunday School of St. John's Lutheran pose on the front steps of the church in this 1928 photo. Davis resident and St. John's member Caroline Miller Pell identified several people in the photo, including herself (age 6, at arrow) with her cousin Annalee Patterson Durant, immediately to the right of her. Photo was taken by the West Virginia Photo Company of Thomas and Davis, West Virginia and today hangs in the narthex of St. John's.

Behold! The Land of Canaan

the trusses to improve acoustics. A manual pump organ was obtained. A large fifty-inch bell was installed in the bell tower, possibly purchased from the Cincinnati Bell Company. The new building was dedicated on September 16, 1894. The church cost $7,000 but, when completed, had a debt of $2,500. Worshipers came from Davis and Canaan Valley and travelled on the railroad from Thomas and Gorman, Maryland, about seventeen miles away. In 1897 a Lutheran church was built at Cortland in Canaan Valley; the Pastor of St. John's served both churches. By 1898 the Maryland Synod Minutes reported that St. John's had 68 communing members with 150 in Sunday School.

The town of Davis continued to grow, but the population was often transient and included many nationalities. Pastors rarely stayed more than a year. According to Pastor Poerschke, "Of the 135 members listed by Pastor Yeakley in 1902, only 19 (or fourteen percent) remained twelve years later. The turbulence and instability of the lumber boomtown created a highly mobile community of varying nationality groups in which most pastors were unprepared to serve. The social instability together with winters that included temperatures which plummeted to -44 degrees in 1898...blowing and drifting snow and three feet thick ice on the Blackwater and Cheat rivers, sorely tried even the hardiest of souls. The limited resources of the small congregation also made continuity of ministry difficult."

The congregation aligned with Holy Trinity in Elkins in 1913, with the Pastor serving both congregations using the train as a shuttle. This alignment made the ministry more stable. Pastor Crissman served for six years (1915-1921), the longest pastorate in the church's twenty-eight year history. During this time, as today, the church was used for community as well as church activities.

The last lumber mill in Davis shut down in 1924; there were no more trees left standing. The population and economy of Davis began a decline; the boom had ended. Population in Davis dropped to 1656 in 1930 and 894 in 1960; school enrollment dropped from 692 in 1920 to 254 in 1962. Over the next forty years the church had five pastors. Membership ebbed and flowed. Lay leadership, especially in the Sunday

This photo appears to capture an early celebration with an international flavor held at St. John's. Thirteen young women posed for photos in the sanctuary and here stand on the front steps of the church. The photographer and date are unknown, although the high-top shoes suggest it took place in the early 1900s. Photo courtesy of West Virginia State Archives.

School, remained strong with Sunday School attendance often over one hundred. The train stopped running in 1942; the Elkins alliance ended in 1945. St. John's aligned with the four-church Aurora parish in 1952. Building repairs continued, topped off in 1961 by excavation of the basement providing space for a kitchen, the first restroom, classrooms and a fellowship hall. Work was mostly done by members.

By 1963 significant changes were occurring that again brought hope to the area. The forest had started to regrow, the land was becoming beautiful again, Blackwater Falls State Park was drawing more tourists (the lodge had opened in 1957), and fishermen, hikers, hunters and skiers were beginning to come to the area. The coal fired power plant built at Mt. Storm led to the openings of two coal mines that meant jobs for six hundred men. President Kennedy's efforts to establish the Appalachian Regional Commission, which focused on this area, were formalized by President Johnson in 1965.

The Synod of the Lutheran Church recognized the possibilities this development created and sent a mission developer, layman "Brother" Daniel Bennett to Davis. Mission developers were generally sent to areas of growth and expansion to develop new congregations, not to assist established congregations; an exception was made for St. John's. "Brother" Dan served the congregation fifteen days a month and focused on both church and community. His community involvement included providing leadership to the Blackwater Civic Association, which established the Blackwater Medical Center with a resident physician, optometrist and dentist; the Tucker County Development Authority, which arranged for the building of Cortland Acres, a skilled nursing home that

opened in 1978 and was originally designed and operated by Tressler Lutheran Associates; and he assisted in the creation of the Blackwater Ministerial Association, getting most area churches working together on common community goals. Lay leadership from St. John's often led worship and kept the Sunday School strong. Sister congregations in other states also provided needed assistance to St. John's and the Davis community. Congregation members, who were also community leaders, helped with community improvements and strengthened St. Johns and found they could make a difference! Brother Dan's personal ministry of visitation among the aged, sick, shut-in, unchurched and new residents soon made his face a familiar one throughout the town. The busy schedule took a toll on Brother Dan's health and he had a heart attack in 1967. He continued with a limited his

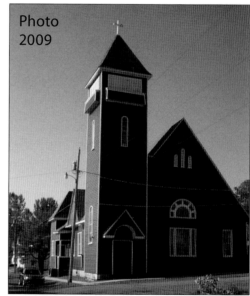

Photo 2009

Postcard photo, Circa 1905

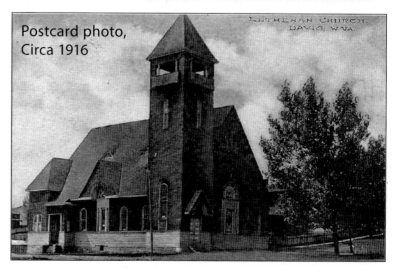

Postcard photo, Circa 1916

ministry until 1969.

Between 1970 and 1981, Davis had a thirteen percent increase in population (from 868 to 979). St. John's renewed its long relationship with the Gettysburg Seminary to provide seminarians, summer residencies and interns for pulpit supply. The seminarians and interns began the park ministries at Blackwater Falls–that continues today– and at Canaan Valley Resort. One seminarian, Fred Soltow, was called as Pastor and helped establish the Tucker County Emergency Squad and served as its second president.

In 1981, the Synod decided to assist the church financially in calling a pastor. Rev. Paul Poerschke came to St. John's and developed a three-fold ministry to church, community and leisure recreation. After three years, he became the Senior Pastor in Davis and residents looked to him as "Pastor to the Community". Pastor Poerschke continued providing strong community involvement and leadership. By 1984 the population of Davis began to drop again. In 1986 the death of lifelong church member Martin Luther "Red" Cooper marked the beginning of a new chapter for St. John's. His bequest of a balsam fir Christmas tree plantation and other assets helped to secure the financial stability of St. John's. On November 16, 1986, the church building was declared an historic landmark by the Tucker County Historic Landmark Commission. Building repairs and modifications continued, including an accessible bathroom on the main floor and a wheelchair ramp.

Pastor Poerschke transferred to a Pennsylvania church in 2000. As always, lay leadership from the congregation continued to be strong. Five congregation members took training to become licensed lay worship leaders and under their leadership church membership actually increased. Major building repairs were begun at this time, including rewiring the church.

In 2001 Pastor Allen Schwarz began as Pastor of St. John's and has continued working with the Blackwater Ministerial Association on community programs including the food pantry, Thanksgiving dinners for the homebound, Christmas baskets and youth activities. Pastor Schwarz added a church phone and website, _www.stjohnsdavis.org._

The active congregation, though small in numbers, is still strong. Three families from the founding members are still serving in the congregation today. On a typical Sunday, thirty to forty members worship in a church that could hold ten times that number. In 2009 more work on the church building was completed: the bell tower structure was stabilized; the walls of the church were sprayed with foam insulation; the windows wrapped in aluminum; and the asbestos siding that was installed in the 1950s was removed and replaced with dark green vinyl siding that is close to the original color. The exterior of the church has regained some of its original beautiful appearance. The new repairs, along with a display of historical items, were highlighted at the rededication on Sunday, June 27, 2010. Now, as was in the past, the congregation looks with optimism to the future and to the next boom period when the pews can be filled.

The town of Davis continues to see changes and signs of resurgence. Tourism is still a key element of success. Blackwater Falls State Park is building new cabins. A few buildings in town are being restored and rebuilt. A new development project may be in the works. Many people return periodically to a town and a church that are special to them; they seem to be called back to this special place. Tourists are still finding the area. The boom optimism continues.

Sources:

Canaan Valley Institute. _A Bit of Canada Gone Astray-Canaan Valley_. Parsons, WV: McClain Printing Co., 2002.

Mott, Pearl G. _History of Davis and Canaan Valley_. Parsons, WV: McClain Printing Co., 1991.

Poerschke, Paul and Allen Schwarz. _St. John's Evangelical Lutheran Church, Davis, WV 1893-2008, History Booklet_. Self-published 2008.

Robinson, Felix. "Davis, West Virginia, Village of Undying Hope." Reprinted from _Tableland Trails_ Vol. 1, No. 1 (Spring 1953): 25-47.

A 1950s view of Maple Grove Lake as seen from Canaan Mountain. Just visible in the trees to the right of the lake is the roof of the restaurant overlooking the lake and owned and operated by Hank and Erma Mallow. Photo scanned from a postcard courtesy of Juanita Pennington Stewart.

Canaan Valley's
Mallow Family *and*
Maple Grove Lake

Sixty years ago Hank Mallow had an idea. Hank was the sort of man who always had ideas, and he was usually pretty good at making them work. He was a successful farmer and dairyman in Canaan Valley and he was always thinking of ways to improve and expand his business to better provide for his family. Hank and his wife Erma owned a farm that sprawled across the Valley that included long road frontage on both WV Route 32 and the old county road known as Cortland Road. The farm was well watered with springs and plenty of high, fertile ground for grazing cattle and growing crops. This beautiful scene was an ideal setting for someone with ideas--and Hank Mallow had an idea.

A small stream rushed through the Mallow farm, carrying fresh water off the east flank of Canaan Mountain year round. Hank began thinking the lay of land would make an ideal site for a dam and a lake. Through that summer six decades ago and into the winter that followed

Hank and Erma developed their idea, discussed it with local contractors, and in the spring of 1952, bulldozer work began in earnest. By fall, a beautiful lake appeared where there had been none the year before. It was the first of its kind in Canaan Valley and Hank and Erma named it Maple Grove Lake.

Today a great deal has changed in Canaan Valley. Although the lake is still a sparkling jewel nestled among the trees at the bottom of Canaan Mountain, it too has changed and, of course, so has the Mallow family. This is the story of the family and the lake and their part in the story of the Valley.

The Early History of the Mallow Family

The story of the Mallow family in Canaan Valley begins with the arrival of two brothers in America in 1749. Hans George and Johann Michael Mallo emigrated from Germany and arrived in Philadelphia on September 15, 1749

Behold! The Land of Canaan

Daniel and Rebecca Lough Mallow pose with some of their children in this photo taken around 1903 at their home on Timber Ridge in Pendleton County. Daniel and Rebecca are seated on the left. Jasper Mallow, the future father of Hank Mallow, is standing third from the right.

as passengers on the ship *Phoenix*. They were soon known by their English-sounding middle names and adopted "Mallow" as the spelling of their surname.

The Mallow brothers traveled south through Maryland and into Virginia looking for work and land. George settled in the Shenandoah Valley near present day Harrisonburg. Michael made his way westward into the wilderness regions of the Appalachians, finally stopping to make his home in Augusta County, Virginia near where the town of Upper Tract is today in Pendleton County, West Virginia. Michael Mallow had decided to make a new home for himself and his new wife in a wilderness populated by more Indians (that is, native Americans) than settlers of European descent

Michael and Mary Miller Mallow were struck by tragedy in their new wilderness home. In an incident known as the Fort Seybert Massacre, there was a series of Indian attacks on settlers, including the Mallow family. Some of the settlers were killed but Mary Mallow and her infant daughter were captured. When Mary returned home more than two years later, she told a terrible tale of the death of the daughter at the hands of the Indians. Despite the hardships of making a life in the wilderness and all the dangers that seemed to surround them, Michael and Mary still succeeded in raising a family there. They had a son Henry who would one day become the great-great-great grandfather of Hank Mallow.

Henry Mallow had many descendents, some of which eventually moved to Ohio or beyond and some who stayed and lived their lives in Pendleton County. Henry had eight children including George Mallow who remained in Pendleton County and raised a family. His son George Mallow, Jr. was born around 1816 and also grew up there. In 1838 George Mallow, Jr. married Rebecca Harman (1819-1853) and moved to the area of Timber Ridge in Pendleton County, a few miles south of the village of

Onego. George and Rebecca lived their lives there and, among their six children, Daniel Bush Mallow was born on April 29, 1850. Daniel Mallow also lived his life on Timber Ridge. In 1872 he married Rebecca Jane Lough (1850-1928), and they are known to have had fourteen children from 1873 to 1894. Nine were girls. On May 1, 1889, twin boys Jasper and Jason were born to Daniel and Rebecca Mallow.

Like many of the Mallow family before him, Jasper Mallow grew up in the Timber Ridge-Onego area of Pendleton County. In 1910, he married Lena Bennett, a local girl he had known since childhood. Soon the first of twelve children was born, Hancel Bennett Mallow. Those following Hancel were Opal, Myrtle, Hazel, Elma, Warren (died in infancy), Velma, Gerald, Forest, Herbert, Roy and Keith.

The Mallows Come to Tucker County

Jasper and Lena Mallow family lived on Spruce Mountain in Pendleton County until America began sliding into a devastating depression in the late 1920s. Desperate for work, Jasper moved his family to the Flanagan Hill area in 1929. Young Hancel Mallow, known as Hank to family and friends, soon found work as a mail carrier making the daily run from Davis to the Red Creek post office located at Flanagan Hill. One of the postal patrons on Hank's mail route was the Lanham family and their daughter Erma soon caught Hank's eye. Hank began to court Erma and they were married in 1934.

A Brief Genealogy of Erma Lanham's Parents

Erma Lanham was the only child of Ulysses Grant "U.G." Lanham and Elizabeth "Lizzie" Heitz. U.G. was born near Buckhannon in 1871, grew up in that area and first married Mary Lantz. A daughter, Pearl, was born, but not long afterward Mary died of tuberculosis and little Pearl was left in the care of Mary's mother. U.G. moved to Davis to find work in the flourishing timber industry, and there he met and married Alice Mason, a young lady from Mt. Storm. U.G. and Alice had two sons, Arthur and Merlin, but Alice died of pneumonia in 1913 at age 30, leaving U.G. to care for the boys. The family today relates that U.G. needed to find a wife to care for his family and he needed to do it without delay. He learned that Joe and Mary Folmer Heitz lived in Canaan Valley and had several eligible daughters that were said to be attractive and "could work like men". U.G. Lanham was soon married to Lizzie Heitz, twenty years his junior, and on November 30, 1916, Erma Isabelle Lanham was born.

Erma lived with her mother and father in their home in Davis, and U.G. worked as a foreman at the lumber mill there, providing well for his family. That is, until the lumber industry began to play out in the early 1920s.

When Erma was six years old, the Lanhams sold their home in Davis and bought a farm in Canaan Valley. They first moved to a home owned by Joe Heitz known as the "Springer Place" while a new home was built for them on the farm. Erma attended Harr School while they lived there then later attended Cosner School after they moved to the farm, finishing the eighth grade in 1928. Recognizing they were too far from town for Erma to attend high school in Davis, it was arranged for her to take high school classes by correspondence for the next two years. Following that, Erma went to live with U.G.'s brother George in Rainelle, West Virginia and attended high school there. It was an ideal arrangement; George was the high school principal.

Ulysses Grant "U.G." Lanham (photo left) around 1919. Young Elizabeth Heitz (photo below) poses in her riding outfit. Known as "Lizzie" to family and friends, she married U.G. Lanham.

Erma 1934

Erma Lanham poses in her cap and gown as she graduated fro Rainelle High School in 193

Hank and Erma Become a Farm Family

Hank and Erma began their married life living in the home of U.G. and Elizabeth Lanham along Route 32 in Canaan Valley. While Hank continued with his mail route, he and Erma carefully counted their pennies and saved their money. Erma helped out by earning a few dollars trekking to Cosner School early each morning to start a fire to warm the building before class started and again afterward to clean. They lived in the Lanham home for three years, during which time their daughter Ruth Louise was born.

In the summer of 1937, America was in the grips of the Great Depression and there was plenty of real estate in Canaan Valley available for sale for only the money the owner needed to get out from under a mortgage they could no longer afford. Just that situation presented itself to the new Mallow family. On July 28, 1937, Hank purchased a tract of acreage along Cortland Road in the Valley. The purchase consisted of three adjoining tracts totaling 190 acres and a large, sturdy farmhouse, all for which he paid $4,205. The sellers were G. Fletcher Harman, his wife Katherine and Fletcher's son George E. Harman and his wife Madeline. Hank's deed of sale for the 190 acres details the terms of payment: $500 cash to the Harmans at settlement and pay off the balance of $3,705 owed by the Harmans on a mortgage held by The Federal Land Bank of Baltimore. Hank's bargain purchase made him and Erma owners of a fine home and farm.

Ruth Mallow on left at age seven holding the hand of her cousin Mary Susan Smith, daughter of Hoye Smith and Louise Heitz Smith. Both Ruth and Betty Mallow grew up as close friends of Mary Susan and her sister Nancy.

Betty Mallow holds onto one of her favorite ponies at the Mallow farm around 1946.

Hank and Erma and little two-year old Ruth moved into their new home without delay that summer of 1937. They were grateful to Erma's parents for the time they lived there while they saved their money, but now they were happy to have a home to call their own. Their new home had been built by John Raese around 1900 when Raese moved there to start an orchard to supply his grocery store in Davis with produce. Raese planted about a thousand fruit trees of all kinds over a period of several years and although some died in the years ahead, many remained to provide an ample supply of fruit for the Mallow family. Raese sold the house and ninety-seven acres to Samuel Harman in 1911, which later passed to his son Fletcher when Samuel died in 1919 and subsequently to Hank and Erma.

Hank and Erma had grown up in farm families and they were well prepared for the task before them to create a new and prosperous life. Over the next fifteen years they did just that. Hank had a good head for business and he undertook a diversity of agricultural initiatives that he thought held promise for making a living for his family. He built a herd of dairy cattle and operated a successful business of delivering bottled milk to local families in and around the Davis area and later on in Thomas. Some years later, Hank converted his dairy business to raising beef cattle. There was ample good ground on the Mallow farm to graze and pasture his livestock, as well as grow plenty of hay, oats and buckwheat.

Hank and Erma's second child, Elizabeth Carol, was born in 1941. Named for her grandmother Elizabeth Heitz Lanham, she was known as Betty to friends and family. She and

Mallow's Maple Grove Lake
Photo Gallery

Hank at the Lake

Hank Mallow poses by the lake in the 1950s while children play in the grass by the lake.

Maple Grove Lake Restaurant in the 1950s. The restaurant and game room were on the first flo rooms to rent on the second floor and a juke box and an area for square dancing in the basement

Mallow's Maple Grove Lake under construction in the summer of 1952. Looking north toward Canaan Mountain, the concrete slab is the spillway and the short brick chimney is the drain. Years later, these structures were removed and replaced with drain and overflow structures visible at the lake today.

Mallow Lake under construction, Summer 1952

Behold! The Land of Canaan

Ruth with horses

In this mid-1950s photo, Ruth Mallow tends two of the horses that visitors could use for riding excursions around the lake. Note the large speaker mounted to the pole on the right of her and at the edge of the lake; wintertime ice skaters were treated to music from the jukebox inside the restaurant.

Betty Mallow stands in front of the lake with her two-year old niece Kaye Bonner around 1957.

Betty & Kaye

Giddy-up!

Erma Mallow poses in a horse drawn sleigh during the mid-1950s when the restaurant at Maple Grove Lake was enjoying great success.

The photo on right was taken around 1958 and appears in Ruth Cooper Allman's book, *Canaan Valley and the Black Bear*, the first of three books Ruth published on the history of the Valley. The photo provides a view of Maple Grove Lake Restaurant from across the lake. The caption in Ruth's book reads, "In front on sleds are, left to right: Lucille Roberts, Jack Roberts, George Allen Spiggle, and Hancel Mallow; standing, Phillip Steyer, Wayne C. Spiggle, William Morrow, Lester Hinkle, Robert Raese, Ann Raese, Betty Mallow, Belmont Cleaver, and Leon Steyer". The photo appears here with the permission of Ruth Cooper Allman.

Chronicles of Its History

her older sister Ruth grew up on the farm with all the fun, adventure, and hard work that goes with being a child in a farm family. The family's horses were an everyday part of their lives, and they enjoyed riding and caring for them along with using them in farm work.

During the 1940s the Mallow farm hummed with activity as Hank and Erma built and expanded it into a prosperous business. It was also the decade in which young Ruth and Betty lost three of their grandparents. A heart attack took U.G. Lanham, at age seventy in October 1941. In May 1943, Hank's mother Lena died of a heart attack at the young age of fifty-three. And then only a few years later in 1947, death took Erma's mother at age fifty-six from cancer. Only Hank's father Jasper lived to see Ruth and Betty grow to adulthood and to know that his large family of sons and daughters had produced more than forty grandchildren and forty great-grandchildren. Jasper passed away in 1967. All four of Hank and Erma's parents are buried at Buena Cemetery in Canaan Valley, a cemetery founded in 1937 on land donated by U.G. Lanham.

Mallow's Maple Grove Lake is Built

In 1951 Hank Mallow had a new idea to expand his farm's potential as a business. He knew that nowhere else in Canaan Valley or surrounding areas was there a lake dedicated to recreation, and he became convinced he could do that on his Canaan Valley farm. In the spring of 1952, Hank hired two local heavy equipment operators, Cecil Canfield and Kermit Butcher, to use their skills as bulldozer operators to push out a big lake bed in a gentle valley on the west side of his farm. Within six months, a beautiful lake glistened in the autumn sun where cattle had grazed the year before. After thinking it over and discussing it with Erma, they decided to name it Maple Grove Lake, reminiscent of that area along Cortland Road where a one room schoolhouse by that name once stood.

Hank's vision for his new creation was more than a lake. Even while the lake was under construction, he began planning to build a restaurant at the south end of the lake. With help from his father Jasper and brother Roy, the three men finished construction of the building in less than a year. It was an immediate hit with everyone.

The building had five rooms for visitors and travelers, a restaurant that served home-cooked meals on the first floor along with room for square dancing in the basement. In the summertime there was swimming and fishing in the lake (stocked by Hank) and horseback riding. A few locals even did some water skiing. In the winter, many came to the lake for ice skating. Hank always cut a hole in the ice to make sure it was safe for skaters and if the wind did not keep the snow blown off, he would use a tractor to clear it. Still, on one occasion Hank had to hop off the tractor when it broke through and sank to the bottom. They found a winch to drag it out, dried it off and it is still in working order today.

Hank and Erma profited from their business at Maple Grove Lake enough that Hank was able to purchase several other farms in the Valley. Even while it was becoming widely believed around 1960 that the state of West Virginia was about to begin acquiring land to create a new state park, Hank purchased farms owned by the Dove, Warner and Craven families with a view toward creating a hunting and recreation preserve in the southern end of the Valley. It was not to be. Hank and Erma lost those three properties during the state's condemnation proceedings to acquire land to create Canaan Valley State Park.

The Lake and Restaurant Get New Owners

Mallow's Maple Grove Lake was a booming business for the family and the community for about ten years. But it was hard work, particularly for Erma who did nearly all the cooking at the restaurant while also maintaining her own family household. By 1960, Hank's interest turned to acquiring other tracts of land in the Valley where he thought there was potential for even greater recreational development than the lake had been. Hank and Erma thought it over and in 1961 they sold the restaurant and all its furnishings along with forty-one acres of land (and lake) to John and Helen Cook for $39,000. The Cooks continued

Behold! The Land of Canaan

to operate the restaurant as a business but hired locals to manage it and its various recreational sidelines. Erma still did some of the cooking on the weekends as an employee of the Cooks. John Cook had career experience in hotel and restaurant management, but Maple Grove Lake did not do well under his ownership. After a few years the Cooks sold out to the local electric utility that was in the process of sweeping up real estate in anticipation of building an electric power generation dam and lake in Canaan Valley. John Cook died in 1969 at only age fifty when he was the owner and operator of Blennerhassett Hotel in Parkersburg.

After the power company bought the restaurant, they used it to store company equipment, but they were soon plagued with vandalism and break-ins. As a result the once-famous Maple Grove Lake Restaurant was torn

Betty and Ruth's children pose in the summer of 1968. Left to right are Kaye Bonner, Linda Bonner, Donna Smigal, Ann Smigal, David Smigal and Kim Bonner. Of the six, David and Kim are the only two who remained to live and work in Canaan Valley.

Hank and Erma Mallow on the right pose in front of their home along Cortland Road in Canaan Valley in 1966. On the far left is Ruth's daughter Linda. The lady holding a hat is unidentified.

down in the late 1970s. Today, if one looks carefully, there are one or two foundation stones ever so slightly visible in the grass where the building once stood. All else is gone.

The Later Years of the Mallow Family

Hank and Erma scaled back the pace of their lives after selling the restaurant and lake. Their daughter Ruth married Kermit Bonner in 1955, and they lived in the Mallow home place until moving to their farm in the Flanagan Hill area where they live today. Ruth and Kermit have three children, Kaye, Linda and Kim, five grandchildren and five great grandchildren. Betty married Alex "Junior" Smigal, and they lived and worked in the Baltimore area and had three children, Donna, Ann and David. Alex retired after thirty years with Bethlehem Steel and the family returned to live in the Mallow home place where Alex died in 1998 at age sixty-six. Betty has five grandchildren and four great grandchildren. A few years ago, she moved to a new home in Canaan Valley and her son David, his wife and two step sons now live in the Mallow home place.

Hank and Erma both lived longer than their respective parents but both appear to have succumbed to a genetic heritage of disease from their parents. Erma died of cancer in 1981 at age sixty-four and Hank died of a heart attack the following year at age seventy-two. Both were laid to rest near their parents in Buena Cemetery in Canaan Valley.

Years later, history proved that the power company never built the electric power dam and lake and the land around Maple Grove Lake returned to private ownership. The acreage that stretches between Route 32 and Cortland Road and includes Maple Grove Lake is now a development of elegant homes surrounding and overlooking the lake. In the years ahead, more homes will surely come to be sprinkled over the wide swath of land that stretches up the hill from the lake toward the old Mallow home. A great deal has changed in the nearly seventy-five years since Hank and Erma paid $23 an acre for their farm. Today the beautiful homes coming to that land are driving prices toward a half-million dollars an acre. Somewhere, it must be putting a smile on Hank's face to know that Maple Grove Lake has been such a great success. After all, it was his idea.

In Appreciation

The author is grateful to sisters Betty Mallow Smigal and Ruth Mallow Bonner for sharing their memories and many photographs and for reviewing and editing the narrative and giving their approval for it to appear as a *Chronicles* feature. Thanks also are owed to Nancy Smith Johnson and Mary Susan Smith Fay for their contributions as part of an interview session with Betty Mallow Smigal. Unless otherwise noted in the captions, all photos were provided courtesy of Betty and Ruth.

Alex and Betty Mallow Smigal (right). Alex, known as *Junior* to family and friends, passed away in 1998. Today their son David lives in the Mallow home place and Betty lives in a new home in Canaan Valley.

Kermit and Ruth Mallow Bonner (left). Kermit and Ruth are lifelong residents of the Canaan Valley and Flanagan Hill area. Today they live on their farm in the Flanagan Hill area.

Pursuits

RECALLING THE STORY OF "TWENTY FEET FROM GLORY"

This story of a balloon race held in June 1928 would probably have been lost had it not been for John R. Goodwin of Morgantown and Ruth Cooper Allman, our preserver of Canaan Valley history.

John Goodwin had heard tidbits about this 1928 event during conversations with the Cooper brothers, James and Stewart. He became intrigued and followed the trail here and in Europe for more than a year. His book, Twenty Feet from Glory, was published in 1970 and is now, unfortunately, out of print although copies sometimes appear on web sites such as eBay.

Ruth Cooper Allman lives here in the Valley and at 93 years old was glad to share her knowledge of this moment in history. She was about 12 years old in 1928 and has some memory of this story's events; in 1983 she wrote an article on this topic for the Parsons Advocate. Ruth has authored three books: Canaan Valley and the Black Bear; Roots in Tucker County; and 50 Years of Seniors: Tucker County High Schools and historical facts.

The writer has tried to find additional information with little success. While "googling", the only "hit" mentioned the Gordon Bennett Gas Balloon Race of 1928. It stated "Launching from Ford Airport in Dearborn, Michigan, on June 30, the balloon Brandenburg flew to a rough mountain top landing in West Virginia." An effort to find a photograph of these gas balloons was also futile. Most images were of 1900 military types and the later dirigibles.

Our focus is upon the *Brandenburg* which carried two reserve officers of the German Air Force and Army. One, a Captain, had been the pilot of a dirigible and the other, a Lieutenant, an artillery officer, both during WWI.

This version of the story, told primarily through photographs, begins as the balloon *Brandenburg* passes over Preston County and enters Tucker County. However, for a better appreciation of the difficulties faced by these adventurers it helps to know more about the balloon, its lifting medium and especially the impact of weather.

The balloon was constructed from a cotton fabric that was coated to prevent the escape of the natural gas which made it lighter than air. It was rounder and larger than our present hot air balloons. A rope netting was used to help retain the shape and to it was attached the open basket holding the aeronauts and all their equipment. They were prepared for cold weather, landings in water, high altitudes and the absence of oxygen; they brought food and water sufficient for several days. They carried maps and a

Twenty Feet from Glory, by John R. Goodwin, McClain Printing Company, Parsons, WV, 1970. This book tells the fascinating tale of the international balloon race that began in Michigan on June 30, 1928 and, for one of the German teams, ended on top of Cabin Mountain as their craft failed to clear the summit.

Behold! The Land of Canaan

1. Photo of Fairfax Stone which marks the source spring of the Potomac River. Photo courtesy of Elliott Ours.

crude altitude measurement device. If the temperatures were high, the gas expanded and the balloon ascended rapidly until cooler temperatures created stability or caused the balloon to descend. While the rising and descending were largely a function of air temperature and updrafts or downdrafts of wind, the horizontal movement of the balloon was totally determined by the often erratic wind direction. Around the sides of the basket were bags of sand which could be hand released and, in a minor way, allow for an increase in altitude. In urgent situations, to drop altitude, gas could be released by a valve atop the bag. Clearly these travelers had little control over their balloon. The weatherman at Ford Field estimated the flight path of the balloons would cross Lake Erie, enter Ohio near Cleveland, move onward to Pittsburgh and across the Virginias toward the Carolinas and perhaps to Florida.

The *Brandenburg* departed about 4:00 P.M. on June 30. After launch, the *Brandenburg* achieved an altitude of about 5200 feet. This varied as the surrounding temperatures warmed or cooled. Between 9:00 and 9:30 P.M. they were crossing Lake Erie. As the air cooled they began to drop sand to maintain altitude. To illustrate the complexities, they drifted into a low pressure area containing a violent down rush of wind. Control was achieved by dumping sand just as the balloon basket bounced into the tops of trees and then began to ascend. During the flight the aeronauts made log entries as opportunity and light permitted. These eventually were published in a German newspaper.

As the sun appeared on July 1, the *Brandenburg* had reached an altitude of 4500 feet. It is estimated that by 3:00 P.M. the aeronauts were closing in on Horse Shoe Run in Tucker County. Here they faced the 3400 foot elevation of Backbone Mountain and, at an altitude of 3500 feet, were nearing our Fairfax Stone (see "A Great Adventure into Primeval Canaan Valley: The 1746 Survey of the Fairfax Line", *Chronicles No. 9*, in *Behold! The Land of Canaan 2009* for more

2. Just to the south of Fairfax Stone you can see Dobbin Ridge in the foreground and beyond Canaan Mountain. At the northerly end of the mountain is Bearden Knob and to the extreme right you will notice knobs of Cabin Mountain. The community of Davis lies along the Blackwater River in a depression between Dobbin Ridge and Canaan Mountain. Photo courtesy of Elliott Ours.

3. As they crossed Pendleton Run, the clouds cleared somewhat and our adventurers could see the rise of mountains just ahead. Canaan Mountain peaks at about 3800 feet, with slight depressions here and there. The town of Davis is about 3100 feet, and as the balloon passed slightly to the north (paralleling Third Street) its elevation was estimated to be 300 to 600 feet above the ground. Sand was released to gain altitude as they approached Canaan Mountain.

4. About 6:00 p.m. the Cooper brothers were near St. John's Lutheran Church and observed the balloon. They believed the *Brandenburg's* altitude was about 700 feet too low to clear Cabin Mountain even if it should go over Canaan Mountain just ahead. They jumped into their father's car and started up old Route 32 to the summit near Bearden Knob. They had lost sight of the balloon and thought it was down on the mountain but decided to continue along Cortland Road in the Valley toward Cabin Mountain. At this time the skies were heavily overcast and a sharp wind was blowing leaves and debris.

From this view of Third Street and St. John's Lutheran Church in Davis, the *Brandenburg* was seen to the left. Note Canaan Mountain ahead and Bearden Knob to the left. Photo courtesy of Elliott Ours.

5. In the foreground is Canaan Valley; the knoll of Cabin Mountain can be seen just beyond the current Timberline ski area. Except for the ski slopes, this must be the scene the aeronauts beheld as they sailed toward the mountain.
Photo courtesy of Elliott Ours.

information about this historic monument). There is a story about a young girl grasping a dangling rope from the balloon and of being dragged a short distance before she was forced to release it. It is not clear where this occurred, but it does indicate the *Brandenburg* was barely above the Valley floor as it headed for the base of the mountain. Mr. J. C. Graham was outside and herding his cattle toward shelter away from the impending storm and had not noticed the balloon. About that time, the Cooper brothers and other cars from Davis arrived.

The *Brandenburg* had been grabbed by the winds and was literally dragged up the mountain banging against rocks and old trees as the aeronauts frantically dropped ballast. Midway up, they were snagged by a tree branch and escaped by sawing through it. But near the summit, the journey came to an abrupt end as a large, dead tree caught several of the dangling ropes – of which one controlled the gas valve. The balloon collapsed. The basket came to a rest on the ground below. The captain escaped injury, but the lieutenant was badly shaken by the bouncing of the basket as they were forced up the mountain

After overcoming initial shock they took stock of the situation and realized it would be very difficult to find their way down the mountain with the growing evening darkness. So they prepared to spend the night here. In his log the captain described high trees around him, parts of which were still alive and others partially falling down and rotten, blocks of granite, tree stumps and shoulder

Behold! The Land of Canaan

Present day Freeland Road would be to the right. Straight ahead, at the base of the mountain, is a large cluster of conifers. The home of J. C. Graham was located here. Graham owned most of the mountain to the summit. To the left is a swale in which Idlemans Run descends. An old logging road, present day Forest Service 80, paralleled Idlemans Run. Photo courtesy of Elliott Ours.

This 2008 photo taken near the Graham farm gives some idea of what might have been seen by the aeronauts. Here you view the forest that is re-grown since the timber industry ended about eighty-five years ago, but in 1928 the terrain of the mountain was largely boulders and dense brush, especially mountain laurel. Photo courtesy of Elliott Ours.

high briars. To their delight they soon heard voices in the distance followed by the arrival of five men. They were the Cooper brothers, the Raese brothers and Jim Browning. The captain's command of English was minimal; the lieutenant had none, and the young Americans could not speak German. Even so, they managed to communicate and descended the mountain together. The aeronauts went with them for the night at the Raese home in Davis.

Early the next day the group returned to the Valley and was joined by J.C. Graham and others. Two workhorses were connected to a sled and began the trek up the mountain. Soon however the terrain became too rugged for the horses. They remained with some of the children. The men cut their way through the brush and trees with axes until they arrived at the balloon. They began cutting and removing the snags and brush which were entangled with the balloon's webbing. After several hours of arduous labor the balloon was rescued, carefully folded and

6. The Cooper brothers drove along old roads across the Valley floor, at an elevation of 3150 feet, toward Cabin Mountain which peaks at 4275 feet. Log entries for the *Brandenburg* indicate it had cleared Canaan Mountain by about 250 feet, and then they knew the approaching Cabin Mountain was a real danger. They began dropping sand to get above the winds and gain altitude for the approaching mountain. It was now about 6:30 p.m. and the *Brandenburg* was seized by a violent vertical downdraft thunder squall; they were now just above the valley floor and rapidly approaching the mountain.

Chronicles of Its History

The aeronauts and their rescuers pose for a picture taken by Walter Raese as they returned from the wreck of the Brandenburg on July 2, 1928. Frank Cooper is second from the left, leaning on the paddle, and his daughters, Ruth, 14, and Elsie, 9, are the two youngsters on the right. One of the aeronauts is sitting highest on the sled and the other is at the front of the sled with both feet on the ground. Photo courtesy of Walter Raese and Mary Jane Raese Moroney.

stuffed into the basket to be rolled slowly down the mountain to the sled. After arrival at the Graham home, the basket and balloon were loaded onto a truck and transported to the train station in Davis for shipment to New York City and later to Germany. After several days with their hosts, the German aeronauts also departed by train for New York.

Mr. Goodwin's work contains several photographs taken in 1928. Of particular interest is one taken by Walter Raese, which appears here with the gracious permission of his daughter, Mary Jane Raese Moroney. Mr. Raese, 101 years old as this was written, lives independently and comfortably in the Morgantown, West Virginia area. This photo shows the rock sled, balloon, aeronauts, rescuers, and children who tagged along for the adventure. Ruth Cooper Allman tells us she and her sister Elsie Cooper Teter are in the picture and that the man leaning on the paddle is her father, Frank Cooper. Paddles were carried in the craft in the event of a water landing, but little thought had been given to preparing for a landing in the wilds of West Virginia.

No evidence remains on Cabin Mountain today of the crash of the balloon *Brandenburg* that caused such a stir here in 1928. Trees, rhododendron, blueberries, ferns and mosses have grown over the landscape erasing the evidence of this interesting event.

Fortunately, the story has not been lost, thanks to John R. Goodwin of Morgantown and Ruth Cooper Allman, our preserver of Canaan Valley history.

Ruth Cooper Allman at home in Canaan Valley today proudly holding the oar her father Frank recovered from the wreck of the balloon *Brandenburg*. Photo courtesy of Friends of the 500th, with permission of Ruth Cooper Allman.

Behold! The Land of Canaan

In this photo notice the open area near the summit, perhaps a natural bald will remain. Canaan Mountain is just visible in the background. Photo courtesy of Vernon Patterson.

REVISITING THE SCENE OF "TWENTY FEET FROM GLORY"

The renewal of our red spruce forest continues here on the lands of the Canaan Valley National Wildlife Refuge. This forest is essential to the survival of the Northern Flying Squirrel, the Cheat Mountain Salamander and other species. Photo courtesy of Vernon Patterson.

A current survey marker located atop Cabin Mountain; earlier maps suggest markers were implanted before 1920. Photo courtesy of Vernon Patterson.

Chronicles of Its History

The Heitz Family and the Legacy of Skiing in Canaan Valley

The view today looking south along Route 32 in the southern end of Canaan Valley. Still visible on the hillside on the east side of the road are the remnants of the ski runs built by the Ski Club of Washington DC in the early 1950s. The **X** on the photo is where the old Heitz home place stood that was used as a ticket window, snack bar and warming hut for the first skiers to come here and pay one dollar to enjoy a day of skiing in Canaan Valley.

Wintertime in Canaan Valley. Snow blankets the landscape of rolling fields, forests, frozen wetlands and surrounding mountains. Anyone who loves snow sports has plenty to choose from in the Valley–downhill and cross-country skiing, snowboarding, tubing and more. It is all here at four great destinations located just a few miles from one another–Timberline, White Grass, Canaan Valley State Park and Canaan Valley National Wildlife Refuge. But amid all the wintertime activity, little notice is given to a stretch of Cabin Mountain hillside, just south of the Canaan Valley State Park ski area entrance. Here, Canaan Valley's skiing industry got its start in the early 1950s when the Ski Club of Washington DC leased a piece of that hillside and opened what they called Cabin Mountain Ski Area. That tiny beginning of commercial skiing occurred because of the spirit and vision of people who thought it held hope for the Valley's future.

Among those people, Canaan Valley's Heitz family and their friend Bob Barton played a critical role in shaping that future. Emily Warner Smith, a granddaughter of the Heitz family, met with this writer and recalled the history of her family and her memories of those early years of skiing in Canaan Valley. Most of what follows comes from those interviews.

The Heitz Family's Roots

Like so many people who came to settle in Canaan Valley, the ancestors of the first members of the Heitz family began their journey in Europe. Family historian Joyce Brenwald Bond documented that her great-great-grandfather, Joseph Heitz, was born around 1838 in an area of France near the border with Germany. He came to America, settled in Meigs County, Ohio, fought in the Civil War on the side of

Behold! The Land of Canaan

the Union, and married Christine Ohlinger in 1866. A daughter, Barbara, was born to Joseph and Christine in 1868 and a son, Joseph, in 1870. The elder Joseph had been in deteriorating health following the war and died in 1872. He is buried in Kennedy Cemetery in Meigs County.

In 1873, the widow Christine Heitz brought her children Barbara and Joseph into a marriage with Simon Young, a widower seventeen years her senior with six children of his own. Christine and Simon eventually had three children of their own: Simeon, Emma, and Edward. They lived the rest of their lives in Ohio.

Young Joseph Heitz, grew up in this large family, and in 1891 he married twenty-seven year-old Mary Folmer. In the next four years, Joe and Mary brought their first three children into the world: Elizabeth, Joseph, Jr. and Ruby. Just as so many young men did to support their families during these years, Joe found work in the timber industry, working in the woods felling trees and moving logs to a saw mill. Meigs County, Ohio borders on the Ohio River, and Joe worked on timbering jobs in both Ohio and West Virginia. As fate would have it, a timbering job brought him to work in Canaan Valley. Apparently he was struck by the beauty of the place–or perhaps by the availability of land at bargain prices. He made several trips back to Canaan Valley and bought a tract of land in the southern end of the Valley. In 1898, Joe and Mary packed their family and belongings into a horse-drawn covered wagon and made their way to their new home.

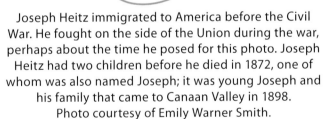

Joseph Heitz immigrated to America before the Civil War. He fought on the side of the Union during the war, perhaps about the time he posed for this photo. Joseph Heitz had two children before he died in 1872, one of whom was also named Joseph; it was young Joseph and his family that came to Canaan Valley in 1898.
Photo courtesy of Emily Warner Smith.

Joe Heitz, Sr. with some of his family and neighbors circa 1910. He is standing in the middle of the group, holding a bucket in his right hand. From left to right are Joe's daughter Ruby Heitz, Caroline Kesner Harr, Caroline's husband Frank Harr (holding shotgun with infant daughter Mabel on chair in front of him), Albert "Ab" Crossland, Joe Heitz, Sr., Jake Harr, young John Cooper (son of Frank and Mamie Harr Cooper), Joe Heitz, Jr. and Connor Simmons. Photo courtesy of Hallie Warner Brenwald.

Mary Folmer Heitz and her pet beside a rock outcrop on her farm in the southern end of Canaan Valley, probably in the early 1930s. Joe Heitz, Sr. below, in the late 1940s. Both photos courtesy of Emily Warner Smith.

The Heitz Family in Canaan Valley

When the Heitz family arrived in the Valley, they moved into a small log cabin that stood on the property along the old county road that wound its way from Davis south to the village of Red Creek, also known as Flanagan Hill. Joe set to work building a large, two-story home that they moved into in 1899. Their family began growing again with the arrival of Christine in 1903, Oscar in 1904, Anna Marie in 1908 and Irene in 1912. Anna Marie was always known as Mary to family and friends.

Joe and Mary Heitz raised all seven of their children to adulthood as responsible and productive citizens. They all went to school through the eighth grade at the Harr School but not beyond that because there was no transportation to the high school in Davis. All the children lived their entire lives in the Canaan Valley area.

By the mid 1930s, the Heitz children were grown and Joe and Mary were enjoying the fruits of their life and a growing number of grandchildren. But tragedy struck as Mary Folmer Heitz suddenly died in early 1937 at age 73 from an untreated infection that started in an open wound on her hand. She was buried at Flanagan Hill Cemetery on February 4, 1937; less than two months later, her husband had her grave opened and the casket moved to the new cemetery at Buena, in Canaan Valley,

A 1913 photo of the four children of Joe and Mary Folmer Heitz born in Canaan Valley; middle front is Irene, Christine on the right, Oscar in rear and Anna Marie "Mary" Heitz on the left. Photo courtesy of Emily Warner Smith.

Behold! The Land of Canaan

on March 24. Buena Cemetery had just been established, and Mary was the second burial there, following Losie Carter Graham who was buried just days before. Joe lived for another fourteen years at the Heitz home place, looked after by his youngest daughter Irene and her husband Hobert Mauzy.

Anna Marie "Mary" Heitz

Along with her six brothers and sisters, Anna Marie 'Mary" Heitz grew up in the big home built by her father when he came from Ohio in 1898. The Heitz home place, which is now gone, was located along Route 32 across from where the Canaan Valley State Park maintenance building stands today. Much like many rural homes of that day, it had no electricity, running water, nor indoor bathroom. But life in the Heitz home was filled with love and plenty of work for the whole family. The children knew from a very young age that each had his or her part to do in the home and on the farm, imprinting on them that indelible work ethic for all their lives.

During Mary's childhood, she was acquainted with Charles Phillip Warner. Charles was five years younger and they attended different schools; he went to Cosner School and she went to nearby Harr School. But the Heitz and Warner families, and others from the Valley, often visited with one another while attending Saturday night dances held at a local gathering place known as "the platform".

As years passed and Mary began to take an interest in young men, Charles caught her eye as handsome and captivating. Those five years of age difference did not seem to matter any longer; Mary was smitten, and they were married in 1933.

Charles and Mary lived in the Warner family home along with Charles' mother Angeline Nine Warner. All five of their children were born there: Flora in 1934, Sarah in 1935, Frank in 1937, Hallie in 1938 and Emily in 1940.

During the early years of their marriage, it was difficult for Charles to find steady work to support his family. He went as far away as Baltimore as a heavy equipment operator and was often away from home for long periods of time. These absences along with Charles' good looks and tendency to have a wandering eye brought the marriage to an end in 1943.

Young Mary Heitz, above left, with some of her friends on a hunting foray circa 1930. Photo courtesy of Sadie Harman Johnson.

Charles Phillip Warner circa 1930. He and Mary Heitz were wed in 1933, a marriage that produced five children but ended in divorce ten years later. Photo courtesy Emily Warner Smith.

Mary Heitz Warner and Her Children Start a New Life

After Mary and Charles were divorced, responsibility to raise the family of five children fully fell on Mary. She moved several times but just could not make ends meet. Fortunately, her father, Joe Heitz, Sr., stepped in and sold her forty-two acres on the side of Cabin Mountain for one dollar–or as Joe would say, "...for one dollar and her lifelong love for him." The family says he had to loan her the dollar. Sitting on the property was an old, but stoutly built, six room house: it had a kitchen and two rooms downstairs and three bedrooms upstairs. The property and home had belonged to Abraham Lincoln Cosner, son of Solomon and Catherine Cosner, the first permanent settlers in Canaan Valley, and had been purchased from him by Mary's father many years earlier.

The old house needed a great deal of work before it would be ready for Mary and her children. The kitchen and bedroom above it had walls that were originally filled with sawdust as insulation, and water had leaked into those walls and rotted the timbers. Again, Mary's family came to her assistance. Her brother Oscar tore the ruined kitchen and bedroom off the house and walled in the open end of the now four-room house. Mary's new home for her and her children had no electricity, running water, nor an indoor bathroom. They stored perishable food in the cold water of a nearby spring, although later

Mary Heitz was known to be able to work as hard and get as much done as any man. Here she is cutting firewood behind her home circa 1950. In the background is the base of the slope that would become the Weiss Knob Ski Area a few years later. Photo courtesy of Emily Warner Smith.

Behold! The Land of Canaan

they did have an indoor cold water spigot piped from the spring and the luxury of a propane gas refrigerator. One of Mary's nieces clearly recalls taking a shower in pure cold water. Bathing was usually a weekly event in a wash tub with water heated on the woodstove.

Mary eventually kept about eight cows and sold milk to the Carnation Milk Co. that ran a route from Oakland, Maryland. She was a capable carpenter and built a number of outbuildings needed to work her property as a small farm—a woodshed, coal shed and meat house. Mary lived in this home for the next fifteen years and all five of her children would reach adulthood and strike out into the world from there.

The only real wages Mary ever earned were as a cook at Cosner School, located along Route 32 in the Valley. From 1946 to about a year before the school closed in 1962, Mary made the daily two-mile walk each way from her home to the school to prepare lunch for about fifty students in the two-room schoolhouse. Mary never owned or drove a car. During all the years that Mary worked at the school, she was an official employee and had Social Security taxes deducted from her salary of about a dollar an hour. In Mary's later years, the Social Security benefits she received were many times more valuable than those little deductions from her wages.

Mary's father died in 1951, at age 81, and was laid to rest in Buena Cemetery next to his wife Mary. Joe's youngest daughter Irene and her husband Hobert Mauzy had stayed at home with him for the fourteen years since his wife Mary had passed away, and in return Irene and Hobert were given the right to live in the Heitz home place the rest of their lives.

Canaan Valley's First Commercial Skiing

The passing of Joe Heitz, Sr. came about the same time as the Ski Club of Washington DC leased the hillside behind their home and opened the Cabin Mountain Ski Area. Several ski club members came to the Valley looking for a place to ski during DC's snowless winter of 1949-50 and, of course, found plenty of it in Canaan Valley. Official snowfall measurements for the

Canaan Valley Snowfall (inches)									
Year	Jan	Feb	Mar	Apr	May	Oct	Nov	Dec	Total
1945	26.1	12.4	8.0	0.0	3.0	0.0	10.3	24.5	84.3
1946	14.5	22.5	3.0	3.2	0.0	0.0	0.0	12.4	55.6
1947	18.0	40.0	39.0	0.0	0.0	0.0	9.0	5.5	111.5
1948	26.0	45.7	1.5	0.2	0.0	5.0	2.0	16.0	96.4
1949	9.0	10.0	18.0	6.0	0.0	0.0	11.2	10.0	64.2
1950	1.0	14.5	41.6	11.0	0.0	0.0	34.3	28.3	130.7
1951	21.0	8.0	33.9	5.8	0.0	0.0	14.0	17.0	99.7
1952	6.5	6.0	18.0	12.0	1.5	2.0	8.0	18.0	72.0
1953	30.5	10.0	22.4	10.8	0.0	0.0	10.0	16.5	100.2
1954	49.4	26.0	24.0	3.0	0.5	0.8	10.1	34.6	148.4
1955	33.5	13.0	7.5	0.0	0.0	0.0	20.5	21.0	95.5
1956	20.0	8.8	21.0	7.0	0.0	0.0	18.4	15.0	90.2
1957	34.0	28.5	15.0	3.0	0.0	9.0	4.0	26.0	119.5
1958	57.0	80.5	57.0	4.5	0.0	0.0	7.5	17.0	223.5
1959	22.0	3.0	26.5	5.0	0.0	0.5	14.0	21.5	92.5
1960	18.0	69.0	73.0	10.0	5.0	0.0	13.0	44.0	232.0

Monthly and yearly snowfall totals at Canaan Valley for the period 1945 to 1960. Obtained from official National Weather Service records, these snowfall data were collected by George Thompson at his farm in the Valley from 1945 to 1956, and by his son Ben in the years after that.

Valley began in 1944 when the weather bureau established a weather station on the George Thompson farm. By the 1950s, the snowfall data from the Thompson's had confirmed what locals already knew—the Valley usually received more than one hundred inches of snowfall annually and much more than that on a few occasions.

When the ski club first arrived, the hill behind the Heitz home place seemed ideal for skiing, and the Heitz family was anxious to make a little extra money from this new skiing business. An agreement was signed between the ski club and Irene Heitz Mauzy. The home was used for selling tickets, a snack bar, renting skis and a place to come in from the cold. Cabin Mountain Ski Area was little more than a cow pasture with a rope tow driven by the rear wheel of an old truck, but people were soon coming by the carloads to try out this sport that was new to a place south of the Mason-Dixon Line.

Bob Barton Teams with the Warner Family

One of the skiers at Cabin Mountain Ski Area in the 1950s was Bob Barton, a newcomer to Canaan Valley. He had a vision of the future for skiing in the Valley and began to work to make it reality.

Bob Barton was born and raised in Virginia, graduated from Princeton University in 1949, spent two years in the Air Force and, in 1952, began visiting the new ski slope at Cabin Mountain Ski Area. He met Mary Warner and her children, and they soon became good friends. It was not long before Bob decided to build a new ski area, and he asked Mary if he could use the hillside behind her home. She agreed, renting it to him for $100 a year, and the work began.

Located on the lower part of the northwestern flank of Weiss Knob, Bob named the new ski enterprise Weiss Knob Ski Area. During the construction phase, materials were moved up the hill on a wagon drawn by a bulldozer. Still, some loads were so heavy that horses were used to get up the steepest sections. In the earliest days of the new ski area, a rope tow was installed on the left side of the slope. Later a T-bar was built on the right side; skiers could take the rope tow to a flat area that was part way up the hill and ski down from there or choose to ride the T-bar from there to the top. For a while, the road up to Mary's house was in such poor condition that skiers parked by the old Heitz home place at Cabin Mountain Ski Area and rode on a horse-drawn

A late 1950s photo taken at the front of Mary Warner's home. Mary is on the left, Bob Barton looking at the camera, Sarah Ann Warner Wolford (Mary's daughter) standing on the porch and her two year-old daughter Peggy next to her. The woman with glasses and long coat is unknown. Bob's snack bar for skiers is partly visible on the hillside above the house. Photo courtesy of Emily Warner Smith.

sled from there to Bob Barton's new ski slope.

Mary's enthusiasm for helping run the new ski area along with her dogged determination to do all the work that needed to be done brought her the nickname, "Mountain Ma". She could chop wood, haul water, shovel snow and do the farm work of any man and still be a good mother and friend. Later on, her children would echo a line from an old country song, "Mountain Ma, she's the law." And she was.

After skiing got underway at Weiss Knob Ski Area, Barton built an attractive cabin to use as a snack bar with the luxury of indoor restrooms. It had a gravel floor and benches and served as a welcome refuge from the cold winds that often roared across the ski slopes. Mary's girls took turns working in the snack bar to earn a little extra money.

These were enjoyable years for Mary's family, shared with others in the Heitz family and with Bob Barton and his friends. Bob helped make improvements to the comfort of Mary's home, including installing running water for the first time. But an indoor bathroom was never built. Even the luxury of electricity did not arrive until the early 1960s. Bob shared many evenings with Mary and her family and friends, often at nearby Pine Ridge Restaurant and beer hall, known to locals as "the platform", where dances were held in the summertime and roller skating on Sunday afternoons.

Bob drove a green Volkswagen Beetle, often turning heads when he folded up his 6'6" frame to get in or out. One evening as Bob was visiting Mary and her family at their home, several people went out to Bob's VW, picked it up and carried it into the woods. When Bob came out to leave, he let out a whoop at the sight that greeted him. Then he laughed and joined with the others as they carried the car from the woods and sent Bob on his way.

Bob turned the tables on Mary with a joke of his own one night. Mary was down at Pine Ridge. Bob scooped up Mary's pet goose and took it with him to the pub, opened the door and pushed it in. It squawked loudly and immediately ran to Mary, all to peals of laughter from everyone there. The Warner family recalls Bob Barton as a likable guy who could take a joke as well as play one on someone else. Everyone liked him.

Behold! The Land of Canaan

A 1950s view of Cabin Mountain Ski Area from the top of the ski slope. The large building at the bottom of the slope is the old home place of Joe Heitz, Sr. and Mary Folmer Heitz, which doubled as a ticket booth, snack bar and warming hut during the ski season. The larger building on the far side of Route 32 is Pine Ridge Restaurant, also known locally as The Platform, a restaurant and pub for locals and skiers. Photo courtesy of Joe Sagace.

A present-day topographic map shows the approximate location of the first two commercial ski slopes in Canaan Valley. Today they are both gone–replaced by the Canaan Valley State Park ski area that sprawls over the area where they were located. The dashed line on the map is the rope tow symbol that cartographers failed to remove from this later edition of the map.

As the 1950s drew to a close, news began circulating that a new state park would soon be built in the southern end of the Valley. Over a period of about eight years, the state of West Virginia began condemnation proceedings against more than thirty landowners to acquire some 1,700 acres of land for the new park. It was clear from the very beginning that the state was determined to include tracts of land on Cabin Mountain as a potential site for a future ski resort within the park boundary. And so it was that the days were numbered for both Cabin Mountain Ski Area and Bob Barton's Weiss Knob Ski Area.

Nearly all the land owners fought the state in court. Even though most eventually received more money for their land than originally offered by the state, the net gain was hardly worth the effort after paying an attorney to handle their case. All records of land transfers from the citizen land owners to the state of West Virginia are in the Tucker County Courthouse and open for public inspection. A check of those records reveals that the 42 acre tract of land on which the original Joseph Heitz, Sr. home place stood and where Cabin Mountain Ski Area was built was sold to the state for $32,500. Mary's tract of land where Bob Barton had built Weiss Knob Ski Area, shown on the deed of sale as 39.3 acres, went to the state for $14,200. In Mary's case, she went beyond fighting the matter in court; it is told that the first time the Tucker County sheriff came to serve her with condemnation papers, she ran him off with a shotgun. Of course, in the end, the state had its way. Mary had to leave the house she and her family had called home for almost twenty years, and Bob had to close his ski area. Bob eventually received a separate compensation from the state for the snack bar building that he had financed and built on Mary's land. In 1959 Bob Barton leased part of the nearby Randall Reed farm and reopened Weiss Knob Ski Area in that new location.

Mary bought a new home near Eglon, West Virginia (about thirty miles north of Canaan Valley) where she lived for several years, often visited by her children and grandchildren. After the Heitz property transferred to state ownership and became part of the new state park, Mary's home and outbuildings were all torn down. Today, the Canaan Valley State Park ski lodge sits on the very site of Mary's home. The same was done to the Joe Heitz home, barn and outbuildings, leaving not a scrap of evidence of those and other homes that had been sprinkled along the west side of Cabin Mountain. The whole affair of the state's acquisition of land for the park sowed a spirit of distrust in "the government" for many of the Valley's citizens who still vividly remember what happened in the 1960s.

In the mid 1980s Mary began suffering from a failing heart and spent time with several of her children, alternating with stays in the hospital in Elkins. She lived the last three years of her life with her daughter Hallie Brenwald in Ohio and died there in 1990. She was buried near her parents, Joe and Mary Heitz.

Bob Barton gave the eulogy at Mary's funeral; afterward he gave the family a copy of the text he read from that day. It read:

A great mountain woman is gone but not forgotten; Marie Warner...Mary...Mountain Ma, my friend and a friend to so many must never be forgotten. Perhaps she was the last of that special breed of mountain woman, physically and morally strong. She had the admiration and indeed, the respect of all of us who knew her and loved her. And there were and are many of us. As we mourn on this sad day let us all give our personal thanksgiving that we were able to walk beside her, or now follow in the footsteps of this wonderful and special person.
Mountain Ma I salute you!
Mountain Ma you are still the law!

Just one year later, in 1991, Bob Barton passed away. The early skiing era in Canaan Valley had ended. The Heitz family had teamed up with Bob Barton (and the Ski Club of Washington DC) to make it happen; their contributions would ensure that great skiing in Canaan Valley was here to stay.

A 1980s photo (left) of Mary Heitz Warner surrounded by her children. Clockwise from lower left: Hallie, Flora, Frank, Sarah Ann and Emily. Photo courtesy of Emily Warner Smith. The Heitz family holds an annual family reunion at Flanagan Hill. All five of Mary Heitz Warner's children posed together here (above) during the 2010 reunion. Left to right are: Flora Warner Carr, Sarah Ann Warner Wolford, Frank Warner, Hallie Warner Brenwald and Emily Warner Smith.

Behold! The Land of Canaan

The cover of a 1957 information brochure shows skiers lined up at the base of Cabin Mountain Ski Area. Note that Weiss Knob is listed on the cover, indicating that Bob Barton had it open that year. The image of the cover is a scan made by Woody Bousquet and posted at DCski.com. DCSki is an independent on-line publication covering outdoor recreation in the Mid-Atlantic region, including the states of Pennsylvania, Maryland, Virginia, West Virginia and North Carolina. During the winter, DCSki focuses on skiing and snowboarding. In the summer, DCSki covers activities such as mountain biking and hiking.

Ski!
CABIN MOUNTAIN, 3,600 FT.
WEISS KNOB, 3,900 FT.

SKIING INFORMATION OFFICE
ALpine 9-4151
1957 SEASON

DAVIS, WEST VIRGINIA

THEN & now

The Weiss Knob Ski Area on Cabin Mountain

Ca. 1960

2010

Bob Barton's Weiss Knob Ski Area was built in the pasture behind the home of Mary Heitz Warner in the 1950s and is the site of the current Canaan Valley State Park ski area. The 1960 photo shows the building Barton built. It had a snack bar, wood stove, benches, tables and even the marvelous convenience of indoor restrooms. Later, when the state of West Virginia took the entire property by condemnation proceedings for the creation of the new park, Barton was paid for the investment he made in the building. Then it was torn down. 1960 photo courtesy of Emily Warner Smith.

A group of hunters gathers in front of the ESSO gas station in Davis with a horse drawn wagon carrying their gear. They are preparing to depart for their trip through Canaan Valley to the Cooper Camp on Brown Mountain.

Hunting
IN THE HIGHLANDS Heritage

White-tailed deer originally ranged over all of West Virginia, but were nearly exterminated by early 1900 due to over-hunting and habitat loss. In fact, the population of most game animals had dropped to the lowest levels ever known at the end of the 1800s. Deer were almost eliminated from Tucker County by 1900, when it was estimated that fewer than 20 deer survived in and around the headwaters of the Little Blackwater River in Canaan Valley. In January 1930, eight deer procured from Michigan were released on the Monongahela National Forest near Parsons. Between 1937-1939, 17 more deer were released in the Flat Rock area of Tucker County. As hunting regulations were enacted, law enforcement personnel hired, game refuges established, and restocking started, the deer population gradually was reestablished. Only one deer was reported harvested in Tucker County in 1923, but numbers steadily increased until a high of 4,254 was reached in 1951.

Conservation Laws Passed

In 1937, the US Congress passed the Pittman-Robertson Act. This act provided funds for states to engage in wildlife restoration. The West Virginia Conservation Commission (the predecessor of WV Division of Natural Resources) initiated a project called the "Statewide Wildlife Survey". One of the first jobs under the survey was to conduct a study titled "The Ecology and Pre-management of White-Tailed Deer". The Canaan Valley area was one of seven areas chosen to study the population, life history, and range requirements of deer.

Aging stations were started in 1949 for researchers to collect physical characteristics data from the burgeoning Canaan Valley herd. The work was carried out under the Pittman-Robertson research project to collect data in order to manage deer herd populations. Data on weight, antler beam diameters, number of

Behold! The Land of Canaan

points, girth measurement, and hind foot length were collected. Results showed that the Canaan Valley deer taken in the Allegheny Deer Region were, on average, the second largest in the state based on physical characteristics. Data also showed that the deer population statewide and in Canaan Valley had recovered at an alarming rate.

In the late 1940s a special doe season was opened in limited areas where the deer population had become so dense that the animals were eating themselves out of food and doing serious damage to farmers' crops. In 1945 the state legislature passed a law allowing for the issue of permits to kill deer damaging crops. By 1949, crop damage became critical in

Preston and Tucker Counties. In Canaan Valley cauliflower and broccoli growers patrolled fields at night to protect their valuable crops. Special permits were granted to farmers allowing them to kill any deer destroying crops.

Up until the 1951 deer hunt season, West Virginia was almost exclusively under a buck law--only bucks with one or both antlers branched were legal. One deer per season was the limit. That year, the state legislature abolished the buck law and substituted one permitting the killing of any deer during the open season. The action was taken on the advice of the Conservation Commission in order to keep the deer herd in a balanced and healthy condition. The stage was set for the first statewide either-sex "hunters choice" season in December 1951.

1951: Nimrods Take Aim

Hunting licenses for the three-day season sold out early in anticipation of the 1951 hunt. Two extra printings of licenses were necessary because the original estimate of the number needed, based on figures for previous years, proved inadequate. Several county clerks exhausted their first and second allotments and sent in requests for additional supplies.

During the three-day season, one of the largest groups of hunters ever converged on Tucker County. The center of activity was Davis and Canaan Valley. *The Parsons Advocate* reported that "literally thousands of nimrods were in the woods and a record kill was set the first day of the season." Davis housed hundreds of hunters in commercial establishments and private homes. All available rooming facilities were in use in Parsons and throughout the county and motorists reported seeing hunters sleeping in their cars along the roadside leading to the hunt country.

West Virginia's first "hunters choice" deer season resulted in a total kill of around 20,000 statewide, according to the WV Conservation Commission. Tucker County led the way that year with 4,254, working out to be a whopping 10.78 kills per square mile.

Deer numbers declined in Canaan Valley following the 1951 season. At about the same time, deer numbers began to increase throughout

Advertisement taken from
The Parsons Advocate
in the early 1950s.

other West Virginia counties and hunters had less reason to travel to Canaan Valley. The annual deer harvest of subsequent years never matched the numbers of the early 1950s.

Remarkably there were no hunting deaths in Tucker County during the 1951 season. However, two hunters were seriously injured when an artillery shell they found exploded. Ralph Korper and Wallace Dean found the shell while deer hunting in Dolly Sods about 12 miles from Davis. This unexploded ordnance was left over from maneuvers conducted during WWII by the Army. Both Canaan Valley and the Dolly Sods areas were used during 1943-1944 as a military training area. The men were examining the shell when it slipped from their hands and exploded. Although the accident occurred in the early afternoon the two injured men lay unattended for three or four hours until other hunters discovered them in the late afternoon. They were taken to the Tucker County Hospital in Parsons. Both recovered.

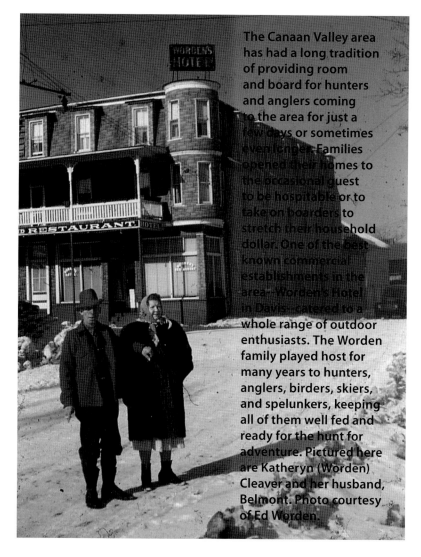

The Canaan Valley area has had a long tradition of providing room and board for hunters and anglers coming to the area for just a few days or sometimes even longer. Families opened their homes to the occasional guest to be hospitable or to take on boarders to stretch their household dollar. One of the best known commercial establishments in the area–Worden's Hotel in Davis–catered to a whole range of outdoor enthusiasts. The Worden family played host for many years to hunters, anglers, birders, skiers, and spelunkers, keeping all of them well fed and ready for the hunt for adventure. Pictured here are Katheryn (Worden) Cleaver and her husband, Belmont. Photo courtesy of Ed Worden.

The "hunter's license" above was issued to R. B. Harr and is dated June 17, 1915. His full name was Raleigh Barker Harr (1853-1931), better known as "Buck' to family and friends. He was born and raised near Fairmont and together with his wife Mary, came to Canaan Valley in 1877 as one of its earliest settlers. Buck and Mary Harr had twelve children, one of which was Idella who grew up to be the mother of 86-year old Dick Harr who still lives in Canaan Valley today. Buck Harr was reputed to be among the Valley's greatest hunters, first to feed his family and later as a guide to visitors who came to the valley to bag a deer or bear. Below Buck's height, weight, etc., it says "...that he is a bona fide resident of this county and a citizen of the United States of America and I am, therefore, this day, issuing to him, free of charge, this RESIDENT COUNTY HUNTER'S LICENSE" It would still be some years before a fee would be charged for a hunting license. Buck's old license shown here was provided courtesy of Dick Harr.

Behold! The Land of Canaan

Growth in Private Property Puts Squeeze on Hunters

The amount of posted land in Canaan Valley increased after 1970 and reduced hunter access and, most likely, hunter harvest. Prior to 1970, almost all undeveloped lands in Canaan Valley were open to hunting and trapping. However, as development spread, especially in the southern end of the Valley, large parcels were posted against hunting. All of Canaan Valley State Park was posted against hunting by 1977 and all of Timberline Resort by 1978. Smaller vacation home developments were posted against hunting at later dates.

Hunter access was limited still further by certain parcels being leased to hunt clubs. The northern end of Canaan Valley was owned by two large land-holding companies--Allegheny Power System and Western Pocahontas Properties--throughout most of the 20th century. These properties have remained open to hunters and trappers, but the Western Pocahontas Properties lands were leased to a private hunting club in 1989 and non-members were not permitted to hunt or trap.

It appears that hunting pressure in Canaan Valley for deer declined during the 1980's and 1990's. This was due to several factors: a decline in deer density, more posted property, and an increase in deer in other regions of West Virginia. Although hunters in Canaan Valley during the 1990's had more days to hunt and higher bag limits, access was more limited and other regions of West Virginia had as many, if not more, deer than did the unposted lands in Canaan Valley. The photos that follow are part of the Martin Luther "Red" Cooper collection and appear here courtesy of his nephew, John Cooper. *Cochran (or Block) Camp, Burley's Camp, Grim Camp,* and the *Cooper Camp* were some of the long established hunting camps that dotted Canaan Valley's landscape. Some still exist today. Cooper Camp was owned by Red Cooper, a farmer and stock owner in Canaan Valley. Red operated businesses in Davis, including Cooper's Restaurant, located at the site of Blackwater Brewery on William Avenue in Davis today. He was an avid hunter and was well known for joining with his friends for visits to his camp during deer season each year.

ACKNOWLEDGEMENT: Research for this article was conducted using a new online archive of past issues--some dating from the late 1930s-- of the *WV Conservation Commission Magazine* and *Wonderful West Virginia.* Individual volumes are available online at <u>wonderfulwv. com</u>. Click on the Magazine Archives' link to search and browse the collection.

Hunter group at the Cooper Camp. Red Cooper (standing, left) appears in the photo. Photo courtesy of John Cooper.

The north end of Canaan Valley was under the ownership of Monongahela Power (later Allegheny Power) for many years. The company acquired the property from Babcock Lumber Company, which had built a logging railroad through the Valley in the late 1910s. Many hunters gained access to the central valley along these rail grades. Notice the two cars in the background. The location appears to be at the north terminus of the Middle Valley Trail, near Glade Run. Cabin Mountain is in the background. Photo courtesy of Veronica Staron.

Improvised log bridges (photo below) were built from the railroad grade remnants in the north end of the Valley to get across Little Blackwater ("Little Black") River just below the Cooper Camp on Brown Mountain. Photo courtesy of John Cooper.

In the photo above, Red and Joyce Cooper (sitting, right) and two friends prepare for the hunt by sighting in their pistols and rifles. Photo courtesy of John Cooper.

Behold! The Land of Canaan

Memories of the Author

As this article was being written the unusually oppressive summer heat had given way to cool nights and the beautiful blue skies so indicative of the coming of fall.

The crunch of the leaves and tang in the air reminded me of my most favorite time of year--when the first few crisp days of fall meant the beginning of the new school year and anticipation of the coming of hunting season. Equal to my memory of that satisfying smell of fall leaves was the scent of gun oil and the musk-filled pockets of my grandfather's old hunting jacket left hanging on the hook since the close of the previous year's hunt season.

My older neighbors--surrogate grandparents--raised a garden which supported them from spring to fall. They shook the trees for apples, peaches, and pears, and every year picked wild strawberries, raspberries, and blackberries. Corn, potatoes, beans, cabbage and other staples grew on their 14 acres. Granddaddy had spent 30 years working far away from home on the B&O Railroad and in his retirement used his land to grow and harvest most of what his family ate and shared with neighbors. Many folks in my neighborhood did the same and prepared for hunting season as a way to pad their pantries and cellars.

Most weekends spent with Grandma and Granddaddy meant waking up to the smell of bread dough rising on Saturday mornings. But during squirrel season Grandma waited for us to return from the woods to start baking. In the early morning light I'd pull down Granddaddy's hunting coat from off the hook and into the woods we'd go. Granddad's beloved but noisy beagles were left behind at the house on these days. I was the one who watched for the tiny prey and pointed them out to Granddaddy. They were hard to hit but patience and a well-placed shot led to a meal not soon forgotten.

Once the game was dressed out it was handed over to Grandma who cooked it in a cast iron Dutch oven. The pot simmered for hours until all the meat easily came off the bones. A thick, rich gravy was prepared from the drippings with tiny pieces of squirrel meat filling the pot. At suppertime we said grace and the hard won meal was served over home-made biscuits. An occasional clink of metal shot could be heard hitting the china plate as we gingerly ate our meals.

It is likely that stories such as these are repeated in households around the region during hunting season. As the season draws near families prepare for visits from relatives and friends. For many it is a time of homecoming, camaraderie, and, literally, one of Thanksgiving. Hunting season--especially deer season--draws families together. Schools close and local economies see an uptick in their revenues. By far the busiest hunt season is deer season and so it is and has been for many years.

RUTH IS 95 !

Canaan Valley historian Ruth Cooper Allman celebrated her 95th birthday on August 28th this summer, marking the occasion in her home by sharing cake and ice cream with friends and family. Ruth has lived here all her life and recalls the years in the 1950s when hunters thronged to the Valley during deer season. Like so many others, Ruth opened her home to hunters to make some extra money during that busy time of the year. Along with a place to sleep, hunters were also served home-cooked meals. On one occasion as hunting season grew near, Ruth knew she didn't have any meat to serve with the meals so she sent her boys out to the barn to butcher an old milk cow. On opening day, there was plenty of meat for those hungry hunters and they all agreed it was the best they'd ever eaten. Photograph courtesy of Friends of the 500th.

An Exploration of

CANAAN VALLEY'S HISTORIC SITES

We Put Down Our History Books and Pulled Out Our Hiking Boots

Tucker County Highlands History and Education Project (TCHHEP) members of the Friends of the 500th gaze down on Canaan Valley from the summit of Canaan Mountain, identifying potential sites for historical investigation. This was part of the preliminary planning for undertaking a survey of historic sites in Canaan Valley in 2007 to assist long range planning activities by the Canaan Valley National Wildlife Refuge. Left to right, Cindy Phillips and Andy Dalton checking a map; Elliott Ours on the big rock; and Bruce Dalton and Bob Hardman scanning the Valley with binoculars.

On a sunny but breezy and chilly Sunday afternoon in the early spring of 2007, two people took a walk along a stretch of the Blackwater River on the Canaan Valley National Wildlife Refuge. Tiny green buds dotted the ends of a few branches, but most trees and other vegetation were as bare as in the dead of winter. It was a perfect day to search for the historic ruins of a landmark that came and went a century ago and was now lost to history. This day's walk was one of a number of times these and other members of the Friends of the 500th would take to the fields and woods of Canaan Valley in the spring and summer of that year looking for remnants of the Valley's historic sites.

A project to survey historic sites was first handed to the Friends by the Canaan Valley National Wildlife Refuge staff when they found themselves facing a problem; they were in the middle of preparing a Comprehensive Conservation Plan (CCP) and a survey of historic sites was a required part of the plan. Without money in the Refuge budget to pay a contractor, the Refuge manager turned to the Friends and asked if they would conduct the survey within the Refuge's 28,000-acre acquisition boundary. The Friends' pack of historians, TCHHEP, seized the opportunity.

TCHHEP, the Tucker County Highlands History and Education Project, which was organized by the Friends of the 500th in 2004, had been a key player in a number of local history initiatives for the past few years. TCHHEP had conducted oral histories with local senior citizens; built a database and digital repository of donated historical photos and documents; erected a plaque to mark where the historic Fairfax Line crossed the Refuge; and written and published historical features in Timberdoodle, the Friends' bimonthly newsletter. The Refuge's request to do the survey sounded like a very relevant, exciting and challenging project; TCHHEP members were ideally suited to do such a survey. And the Refuge wanted it completed in just four months.

Work immediately got underway to decide how to do the survey and which potential historic sites should be included. After studying the task, seventy-six sites were identified including old homesteads, timber industry camps, splash dams, railroad grades, fire towers, hunting camps, quarries, cemeteries, roads, schools, old survey markers, abandoned bridges, old military training fortifications and a possible stand of virgin trees.

Explorations on foot in the weeks that followed were variously conducted by Bruce and Andy Dalton, Julie Dzaack, Bob Hardman, Dave Lesher, Elliott Ours and Cindy Phillips. They did the fieldwork of making notes, taking photographs and researching existing written documents about the sites. Summarizing a large volume of data in a format prescribed by the United States Fish and Wildlife Service, a compendium of site locations with descriptions and information relating to historical significance was delivered to the Refuge manager on July 2, 2007. A great deal

In the spring of 2007, TCHHEP's historic site explorers stand on big rocks along Canaan Loop Road on Canaan Mountain where Canaan Lookout Fire Tower stood from the 1920s to the 1940s. All that remains of the tower today are the remnants of the concrete and steel anchors (arrow) that secured the tower to the rocks. Left to right are Cindy Phillips, Andy Dalton, Bruce Dalton and Elliott Ours.

Chronicles of Its History

New and old photos, taken from the same perspective, of the site of a splash dam in Canaan Valley. At the bottom is an enlargement of a portion of the old photo (see dashed box) that clearly shows the dam stretching across the Blackwater River. Note also the opening in the middle of the dam where water was released, carrying logs downstream to the sawmill in Davis. A careful search of this site today reveals there are still a few decayed remnants of the logs that once made up the base of the wooden dam. Old photo courtesy of Ruth Cooper Allman, provided to her by Ben Thompson who held the original photo in his collection and in that of his father George B. Thompson.

had been accomplished in a short time, and TCHHEP was proud of its work. Still, it was evident that more thorough research and analysis was needed for many of the sites to fully understand and explain their historical significance.

As requested by the Refuge, the final report was a one-of-a-kind product. No copies were retained by members of the Friends who pledged to take all reasonable measures to protect the release of survey data, which would reveal the location of sensitive sites without the expressed consent of the Refuge manager.

Ultimately, the project came to be a catalyst to collect and analyze more information, much of it from obscure sources, and to integrate it into future studies and reports. But the labor that had gone into this project gave the Friends a renewed appreciation of the founding of the Valley, of the first families who arrived in the 1860s, and of the hearty timber men, miners and families who arrived with the railroads in the 1880s and who braved the deep winter snows, frigid cold, dense forests and wild animals to farm, work and live here.

On that chilly spring afternoon along the Blackwater River in 2007, the two TCHHEP members on their hunt for history had been given permission by the Refuge to leave designated trails and were trudging along the muddy bank of the river looking for a splash dam built around 1890. Splash dams were used in the early years of the timber industry to help in the process of moving logs to the sawmill in Davis. A splash dam was built of logs and timbers and erected in the river to create a holding pond for water and for logs that were cut and dragged there from the woods. When a sufficient number of logs were in

Behold! The Land of Canaan

the pond, a gate in the middle of the dam was opened, carrying a rush of water and the logs down the river to the mill. This event was called a *splash*.

In its day, a splash dam was very useful under most circumstances. However, it had the serious shortcoming of being nearly worthless when the river was frozen in winter and again during summer droughts when the river flow was very low. Later, when railroad lines were built into Canaan Valley, splash dams were abandoned and left to decay and swept away by the river.

This day, the two TCHHEP explorers had the benefit of several clues where to look for the site of the long gone splash dam. One was an oral history with then 91-year old Ruth Cooper Allman who had been to the site as a youngster and had described its location. The other was a photo of the splash dam taken around 1905, a copy of which was also provided by Ruth.

After an hour or so of slowly walking upstream, repeatedly checking the photo, and even making a cell phone call to Ruth to help clarify some of what she had said, suddenly they realized...they found it! The bend in the river and the profile of Cabin Mountain in the distance were the only features that had not changed. The terrain, naked of trees a century ago, was now covered with mature growth that almost completely hid the site from view. But it was unmistakable. And much to their surprise, a closer inspection of the spot where the dam had stood even showed a few ghostly shapes of remnants of the logs that had been submerged in the river at a base of the dam. "Eureka!" rang out from that isolated spot in Canaan Valley.

In Ruth Cooper Allman's book, Roots in Tucker County (McClain Printing, 1979), she writes about Charles Samuel Teter (1892-1976) who worked the logs on this very splash dam when he was a young man. With Ruth's permission, here is some of what she wrote about Charley Teter:

He went to work in the lumber woods as a young man and in his own words describes: "The first public work I ever did was driving logs on the Blackwater River. I rode the logs in the river and put them where they were supposed to go. Squire Collins was the foreman. I was only 15 years old

when he hired me (about 1907). The Thompson Lumber Company built a dam on the Blackwater River in Canaan Valley and when full the gates were open to a width of eight feet."

"The men would try to keep the logs singled out as they went through the gates. I remember once when I lost my balance and would have went through the gates, but lucky for me Collins was close and jerked me back to safety. I would surely have been killed in that huge mass of logs if I had gone through."

So there we stood where a century before a brief drama had been played out and a young man's life saved. It must have been a great adventure for him to walk the logs and be part of the sounds and spectacle of a splash. For us, it had been a great adventure to visit this special place, and we knew there would be more such visits to the Valley's historical sites in the months and years ahead.

Another stop by the TCHHEP historic site explorers was the site of the Amby and Sarah Dolly Harper home along Cortland Road. The home is gone, its location marked only by the crumbling remnants of a foundation and a grove of aspen that now hide the spot from view from the road. Here TCHHEP members Julie Dzaack and Bob Hardman inspect the old springbox that remains nearby to where the home stood. Amby and Sarah Harper were parents of eight children, one of which was Dolly Harper. Dolly was a homicide victim at the hands of Thomas Jefferson Sites on May 23, 1931. See "Canaan Valley Scene of Fatal Shooting" in Volume one of *Behold! The Land of Canaan*, published by Tucker County Highlands History and Education Project, 2009.

About the Authors

Elliott Ours made lasting contributions in the years he served as president of the Friends of the 500th. His interest in local history was the catalyst that led to the founding of TCHHEP, and he subsequently made contributions to both volumes one and two of this book. Elliott passed away in 2009 and is remembered in the dedication of this book.

Bruce and Andy Dalton are both members of the Friends of the 500th serving on the board of directors and as founding members of the Tucker County Highlands History and Education Project (TCHHEP). Bruce and Andy first came to Canaan Valley on their honeymoon in 1976. Upon retirement from careers in education in 2004, the Daltons built a home and became permanent residents of Canaan Valley. Andy says she will never tire of the beauty of the area and its wonderful people. Bruce is a native Virginian and says history and snow have always been high on his list of interests.

Debra Lucille Harr was born and raised in Petersburg, WV. She and her brother Gene spent time on the Wolford farm in Canaan Valley as children and young adults. Debra graduated from Petersburg High School in 1964 and earned a doctorate in education at WVU, joining the WVU School of Nursing faculty in 1975 where she served as an associate professor and initiated the parish nurse program. She retired in 2005 and currently makes her home in Morgantown, WV.

Janice Hardman grew up in Clarksburg and came to love Canaan Valley in 1946 when her father and grandfather bought land in the Canaan Heights area. She has enjoyed the history of the area, sharing stories with old and new friends and volunteering in several events. Janice has traveled to many states and countries throughout her life but always loves coming back to the mountains of West Virginia. Her three sons also love the area and visit bringing grandchildren and great grandchildren. Janice resides with her husband Bob in Bridgeport, WV.

Dave Lesher retired to the Canaan Area in 2001 after a career with the federal government. He has been actively involved with the Friends of the 500th since 2003 and is a founding member of TCHHEP. Dave's interests have focused on the climate and cultural history of Canaan Valley, and he has written a number of articles and self-published a book on these topics. He and his wife Nancy make their home in Canaan Heights.

Dave Miller first visited the Canaan Valley region in 1981 shortly after moving to West Virginia with his wife Debbie. Dave and Debbie established a vacation residence in the Valley in 1996, which they made their permanent residence in 2009. Both Dave and Debbie are retired PhD chemists with a passion for the outdoors. Dave has an interest in understanding the interconnections between natural and human history and how it affects our modern way of life.

Chuck Nichols is a member of the Friends of the 500th and recently joined in the work of the Tucker Highlands History and Education Project. He first came to Canaan Valley in the early years of White Grass Ski Touring Center then moved here permanently in 1985. He has performed as a local musician, actor and storyteller. Chuck makes his home near Flanagan Hill where working with horses is among his many interests.

Cindy Phillips is a member of the Friends of the 500th and is very active in its history and education projects. A ninth generation West Virginian who now lives in Canaan Valley, she is a member of the Tucker County Historical Society and the Tucker County Historic Landmark Commission. Cindy authored the book, *Images of America: Tucker County*, a pictorial history of the county.

Behold! The Land of Canaan

Index

A

Acadian Mountains 63
Adopt-a-Trail 8
Alford, Barbara (Harr) 53, 54, 58
Allegheny Highlands 2
Allegheny Power System 107, 108
Allen, Jag 11
Allman, Ruth (Cooper) 11, 13, 16, 18, 23, 37, 42, 70, 73, 83, 88, 92, 109, 112, 113
Alpine Festival 26
anglers 50
anticlines 64
A&P grocery store 52
Appalachian Basin 63, 65
Appalachian Mountains 62, 63, 64, 65, 66
Appalachian Regional Commission 75
Archives of West Virginia University 10
Arnold, Jim 55
artillery shell 106
Ashtola, Pennsylvania 15
Auer 4
Augusta County, Virginia 79
Austrians 15

B

Babcock 11, 12, 13, 14, 16, 17
Babcock Lumber Company 13, 14, 108
Backbone Mountain 89
Back Hollow Road 40, 44, 64
Baer, Margaret 33
Baltimore & Ohio Railroad 73, 109
Barker, David 34, 35
Barker, Lavina 34, 35
Barton, Bob 94, 99, 100, 101, 102, 103
Battle of Corricks Ford 27
Beall, Roscoe "Ronnie" 26
Beall, Roscoe, Sr. 24

Bearden Knob 71, 89, 90
Bearden Knob Fire Tower 69, 71
Beaver Creek 14
Beaver Creek Lumber Company 11, 15, 74
Behold! The Land of Canaan 8, 60
Bell, Elizabeth 2
Bell, Frank J. 2
bell tower 75, 77
Ben's Old Loom Barn 60
Berea College 30
Berkeley County, WV 35, 47
Blackwater Anticline 64
Blackwater Avenue 72
Blackwater Boom and Lumber Company 11, 19
Blackwater Brewery 107
Blackwater Canyon 13
Blackwater Civic Association 76
Blackwater Falls 17, 64, 66, 77
Blackwater Falls State Park 38, 39, 56, 75
Blackwater Hotel 11
Blackwater Lumber Company 19, 20, 74
Blackwater Medical Center 76
Blackwater Ministerial Association 76, 77
Blackwater River 1, 11, 18, 19, 72, 75, 89, 111, 112
board feet 13
"Bob Ridley" 18
Bond, Joyce (Brenwald) 94
Bonner, Kaye 83
Bonner, Linda 85
Bonner, Kim 85
Bonner, Ruth Louise (Mallow) 81, 83, 86
Bonner, Kermit and Ruth (Mallow) 86
Bousquet, Woody 103
box factory 14
Brandenburg 88, 89, 90, 91, 92

Brenwald, Hallie (Warner) 26, 95, 102
broccoli 105
Browning, Jim 91
Brown Mountain 104, 108
Brown, Ron 24
Buckhannon, WV 58, 80
buck law 105
Buena Cemetery 1, 43, 96, 99
Buena Chapel 45, 59
Burger 11
Burley, John 16
Burley's Camp 107
Burnside stove 27
Butcher, Kermit 84

C

Cabin Mountain 1, 2, 4, 39, 55, 64, 66, 67, 88, 89, 90, 91, 92, 93, 94, 101, 102, 108, 113
Cabin Mountain Ski Area 55, 58, 94, 99, 100, 101, 103
Calebaugh, Ed 68, 69, 70
Calebaugh, Fred 68, 69
Camp 70 5, 68
Camp Lee, VA 53
Canaan Heights iv, 1, 68, 69, 71
Canaan Heights Road 68
Canaan Lookout Fire Tower 71, 111
Canaan Loop Road 67, 70, 71, 111
Canaan Mountain 39, 64, 66, 67, 69, 71, 78,82, 89, 90, 91, 93, 110, 111
Canaan Valley 1, 2, 4, 13, 17, 18, 22, 24, 27, 28, 32, 33, 36, 37, 38, 39, 41, 42, 44, 47, 48, 49, 50, 51, 55, 56, 59, 60, 62, 63, 64, 65, 66, 67, 68, 71, 73, 75, 78, 80, 88, 104, 106, 107, 109, 110, 111, 112, 113
Canaan Valley and the Black Bear 88

Index

Canaan Valley National Wildlife Refuge ii, 1, 5, 17, 93, 94, 110, 111

Canaan Valley Resort State Park 23, 28, 30, 50, 57, 58, 77, 94, 97, 101, 102, 103, 107

Canaan Valley State Park ski area 23, 25

Canaan Valley Volunteer Fire Department 37

Canfield, Cecil 84

Carnation Milk Company 54, 55, 99

Carr, Flora (Warner) 97, 102

Casablanca 53

cattle 16

cauliflower 29, 105

Charleston, WV 38, 73

Cheat Mountain salamander 93

Cheat River 75

Chesapeake & Ohio Railroad 73

Christiana, DE 34

Christmas 50

Chronicles of TCHHEP 8

Cincinnati Bell Company 75

Civilian Conservation Corps 38

Civil War 36, 94

Clarksburg, WV 3, 70

Cleaver, Belmont 83

Cleaver, Belmont and Kathryne (Worden) 106

Cleveland, OH 89

climate 65, 99

Cluss Lumber Company 37

Cochran (or Block) Camp 107

Collins, "O.B." 25

condemnation 23, 56

Confederate Army 18

Cook, John and Helen 84

Cooper Camp 104, 107, 108

Cooper, Fred 16

Cooper, George Franklin "Frank" 42, 92, 95

Cooper, Henry Jackson 37, 42

Cooper, James and Stewart 88, 90, 91

Cooper, John 42, 95, 107, 108

Cooper, Joyce 108

Cooper, Linda 56

Cooper, Mamie (Harr) 95

Cooper, Martin Luther "Red" 77, 107, 108

Cooper's Restaurant 107

Cortland 17, 75

Cortland Acres 76

Cortland Cemetery 42, 54, 58

Cortland Road 28, 30, 37, 58, 78, 81, 86 90

Cosner, Abraham Lincoln 98

Cosner, Catherine (Schell) 47, 98

Cosner Chimney 6

Cosner, Ruth Ann 56

Cosner School 56, 80, 97, 99

Cosner, Solomon 18, 47, 98

Cosner, William Henry Harrison 37

Coviello, Jean (McBee) 44

Craven family 84

Crossland, Albert "Ab" iii, 1, 24, 27, 49, 95

Crossland Cemetery 27

Crossland, Clara (Burdette) 27

Crossland, Clyde 26

Crossland, Edward 27

Crossland, Elizabeth 27

Crossland, Thomas 27

Crossland, William 27

Crossland, Howard 27

Crossland, George Thomas "G.T." 22, 27

Crossland, Howard 27

Crossland, Nile 27

Crossland, Provey Jane "Poppy"(Yoakum) 22

Crossland, Selena 27

Crossland, Syminthy 27

Crossland, Thomas Jefferson 27

Crossland, Victoria 27

Crossland, William 27

Crossland, Thomas 27

Cumberland, MD 28

Cuppett, Judge D. E. 24

D

Dalton, Andy v, 110, 114

Dalton, Bruce v , 110, 114

Davis Cemetery 43

Davis City Times 73

Davis Coal and Coke Company 17

Davis, Henry Gassaway 11, 18, 72

Davis High School 51

Davis, Rebecca (Harding) 39

Davis, Thomas Beall 11, 72

Davis, William 11, 72

Davis, WV 1, 2, 8, 10, 11, 12, 15, 17, 18, 25, 37, 38, 39, 55, 60, 72, 73, 79, 80, 104, 105, 107

Dearborn, MI 88

Deckers Creek 35

Decker, Thomas 35

deer 104, 105, 106, 107, 109

Deerfield 58

Degler, Katherine 43

Delaware Indians 35

delivering bottled milk 81

Detroit, MI 4

Dobbin Ridge 89

Dolly Sods 64, 71, 106

Douglas, WV 11

Dove Farm 84

draft board 53

Dry Fork 60

Durant, Annalee (Patterson) 74

Durbin, WV 72, 73

Dzaack, Julie v

E

East Germany 3

Index

Eastham, Benjamin Franklin and Lucy Eliza (Browning) 18
Eastham, Mary "Molly" (Reid) 1, 18, 21
Eastham, Robert W. iii, 1, 18, 19, 20, 21, 37, 73
Eglon, WV 102
Electricity 50
electric light plant 17
electric streetlights 74
Elk Garden, WV 2, 37
Elkins, WV 11, 45, 72, 75, 102
English Common Law 24
Eugene K. Harr Theatre 30

F

Fairfax Avenue in Davis 73
Fairfax Line 89, 111
Fairfax Stone 88, 89
Fairmont, WV 35, 36, 37, 39, 44, 48
Fansler, Homer Floyd 20
Fifth Grade Connections 5
Filler, Mary Ann 55
Flanagan family 31
Flanagan Hill 41, 43, 51, 52, 53, 54, 79, 86, 96, 102
Flanagan Hill Cemetery 96
Flanagan Hill Community Center. 59
Flanagan Hill School 51
Flanagan, Robert 37
Fletcher, Sarah (Thompson) 60
Florida 58
Ford Field 88, 89
forests 65
Fort Knox, KY 54
Fort Leonard Wood, MO 53
Fort Seybert massacre 79
Fourth Street in Davis 73
Fowler map 72
Fowler, Thaddeus Mortimer 12
Freeland, James 18
Freeland Road 5, 40, 68, 91
Freeland Trail 5, 6

Free Methodist Church 73
Friends of the 500th i, ii, 110, 111
frost hollow 65

G

Garnett, General Robert S. 22
Garretson, Catherine 35
gas well 45
German Air Force and Army 88
Germany 53
Gettysburg Seminary 73, 77
Gibraltar 54
Gibson, Milford 24
Gill, Frances (Calebaugh) 68, 70
Gill, Harlan 1, 68, 69, 70
Glade Run 108
Glamorganshire, Wales 34, 35
Glenville, WV 45
Goff, Cecil 23
Good, Jim 23, 25, 26
Goodwin, John R. 88, 92
Gordon Bennett Gas Balloon Race 88
Gorman, MD 75
Goughnour, Sam and Amy 68
government spring 70
Graham farm 68
Graham, J.C. 90, 91
Graham, Losie (Carter) 97
Grant County Library 30
Grant County, WV 13, 14, 22, 28
Great Depression 42, 60
Greenbrier 66
Greenbrier limestone 67
Greider brothers 73
Grenville Mountains 62
Greyhound bus 52
Griffith, Mary Elizabeth 37, 41
Grim Camp 107
Grit newspaper 25
Gruden, Josephine 59
Guthrie, Keith 21

H

Haar family 33
Haar, Hans Jacob 33
Hagerstown, Maryland 11
Hampshire County, WV 10
Hardman, Bob 110, 111
Hardman, Janice (Gill) 1, 68, 69, 114
Harman Brothers Construction Company 50
Harman, G. Fletcher 81
Harman, G. Fletcher and Katherine 81
Harman, George E. and Madeline 81
Harman, Samuel 81
Harman, Rebecca 79
Harper, John 37
Harper, Pauline 43
Harpers Ferry 22
Harper's Magazine 39
Harr, Ada 23
Harr, Baley 40, 43, 44, 46
Harr, Bertha 40, 43, 44, 48, 50, 51
Harr, Bessie Carrol iii, 1, 28, 29, 30, 41, 42
Harr, Betty 42
Harr, Brady 40, 43, 51
Harr Brothers' Farm 54, 56
Harr, Carl and Maria (Partosa) 31, 58
Harr, Carney Jackson "Jack" 42
Harr, Caroline (Kesner) 95
Harr, Carrie 37
Harr Cemetery 40, 43, 44, 47
Harr, Charles 37, 42
Harr, Charlotte 39, 42
Harr, Constance 37
Harr, Cora 37, 42
Harr, Curtis 47
Harr, David 33, 34, 46
Harr, Debra Lucille 28, 29, 30, 31, 40, 41, 42, 114
Harr, Delarie (Hanger) 28, 29, 41, 42, 46

Index

Harr, Dorothy 29, 41, 42
Harr, Earl 41
Harr, E. Debs and Lucille "Tippy" 28
Harr, Edith 46, 48
Harr, Eleanor 37
Harr, Eliza 34
Harr, Elizabeth "Aunt Betty" (Cosner) 47
Harr, Eugene Debs 28, 29, 30, 41, 42
Harr family 31
Harr, Frank 37, 43, 95
Harr, Fred 42
Harr, Frederick 33
Harr, Guy 41, 42
Harr, Herbert Milton 37, 43
Harr, Herbert Milton, Jr. 37, 39
Harr, Hester 28, 41, 42
Harr, Ida 34
Harr, Idella 1, 32, 33, 35, 37, 38, 43, 45, 46, 47, 54
Harrisonburg, VA 47
Harr, Jacob "Jake" 34, 39, 40, 41, 46, 49, 95
Harr, James 34, 56
Harr, James "Jimmie" 46, 58
Harr, James Merrick 33, 34, 35, 36, 39, 40, 41, 45, 46, 47, 48, 49, 53, 54
Harr, Jane 34
Harr, Jimmy and Marylyn (Hostetler) 58
Harr, Joe 54, 56, 58
Harr, John 33, 34, 39, 42, 46
Harr, John Henry 33
Harr, John Rufus 28, 29, 40, 41, 42, 46
Harr, Joseph 46, 47, 50
Harr, Lavina (Barker) 36
Harr, Lloyd Carl 44, 46, 47, 54, 55, 56, 58
Harr, Louisa 34
Harr, Lucetta 39, 40, 42, 46
Harr, Lucinda 34
Harr, Mamie 39, 42, 43

Harr, Mary Jocelyn "Jo" (Raines) 36, 38, 39, 42, 43, 44, 46, 48, 50, 51, 52, 53, 56, 58, 106
Harr, Mary Opal 47
Harr, Mathias 33
Harr, Morgan 46
Harr, Odessa 40, 43
Harr, Ole 37
Harr, Phyllis 47, 58
Harr, Priscilla 34
Harr, Raleigh "Buck" 31, 34, 35, 36, 37, 38, 40, 43, 44, 48, 56, 106
Harr, Rebecca 37
Harr, Richard "Dick" Milton 1, 26, 31, 32, 33, 34, 35, 36, 37, 40, 44, 47, 51, 53, 55, 56, 57, 58, 106
Harr, Rufus 34
Harr School 28, 38, 49, 80, 97
Harr, Seymour 34, 36, 39, 40, 42, 46
Harr, Simon 33, 36
Harr, Socrates "Crate" 34
Harr, Sylvester 46, 47
Harr, Virginia 37
Harr, Warren 37, 42, 44, 46
Harr, Warren and Katy 46
Harr, Zimri 33, 34, 35, 36
Hedrick family 31
Hedrick, Kate 59
Heitz, Barbara 95
Heitz, Bill 52
Heitz, Christine 96
Heitz, Christine (Ohlinger) 95
Heitz, Elizabeth 95
Heitz family 55
Heitz, Irene 96
Heitz, Joseph (b. 1838) 1, 94, 95
Heitz, Joseph Sr. (b. 1870) 95, 96, 98, 101, 102
Heitz, Joseph "Toots" Jr. (b. 1894) 1, 22, 23, 26, 27, 49, 95

Heitz, Mary (Folmer) 80, 95, 96, 101
Heitz, Oscar 50, 96, 98
Heitz, Ruby 95
hemlock 14
Hendricks, WV 13
Hinkle Funeral Home 25
Hinkle, Lester "Buck" 25, 26, 83
Hinkle, Russell 50
Holt, Homer 21
Hopemont Sanitarium 43
horses 12
Horseshoe Bend 64
Horse Shoe Run 89
Huddersfield, England 22
"hunters choice" season 105
hunting 1, 104
hunting licenses 105
hunting season 109

I

Idlemans Run 91
Imboden, General 18
Imhoff, May Ann 44
Internal Revenue Service 23, 25, 26
Inwood, WV 35
Italy 53

J

Japan 54
Johnson, Nancy (Smith) 23, 27, 86
Johnson, President Lyndon B. 76
Johnson, Reva Jean 56
Johnson, Sadie (Harman) 97
Johnston, Willard 52
Johnstown, PA 15
Jones, Colonel William E. 18
Jones family 68
Jordan, Bessie 21

Index

K

Kaemmerling, Sarah Maude
    (Thompson) 23
Kennedy Cemetery 95
Kennedy, President John F. 75
Kenyon, Ralph B. 20
kerosene lamps 50
Kesner, Caroline 43
kindling wood factory 14, 15
King, Andrew 6
King, Michele (Ours) 4, 8
Kingwood, WV 18
Kitzmeyer, Pastor J.F.W. 73
Kramer 16
Kyle, Lucille 42

L

Lake Erie 89
Lake Louise, Alberta 4
Lambert, Dr. D. O. 10
Laneville Road 67
Laneville, WV 41, 55
Lane, Warden 56
Lang, B.O. 13
Lang, Bretzel 13
Lanham, Alice (Mason) 80
Lanham, Arthur 80
Lanham, Elizabeth (Heitz) 80
Lanham, George 80
Lanham, Mary (Lantz) 80
Lanham, Merlin 80
Lanham, Pearl 80
Lanham, Ulysses Grant "U.G."
    and Elizabeth (Heitz) 80,
    81
Lantz, Mary 80
Lawrence family 31
Leadmine, WV 58
Lesher, Dave v. 111
Lewisburg, WV 43
Lewis, Martha (Crossland) 27
Liberty ship 53
Library of Congress Maps
    Collections, 12
Lime Rock 13
limestone 1, 63, 64, 65, 66

Linger, Constance "Connie" 38,
    43
Little Blackwater River 108
Love, Mr. 68
lumber camps 60
Lumberport, WV 39
Luther, Martin 74

M

Mallo, Hans George 78
Mallo, Johann Michael 78
Mallow, Daniel and Rebecca
    (Lough) 79
Mallow, Daniel Bush 79
Mallow, Elma 79
Mallow, Erma (Lanham) 1, 30,
    78, 79, 83, 84, 85, 86
Mallow, George 79
Mallow, Gerald 79
Mallow, Forest 79
Mallow, Hancel "Hank" 1, 30,
    78, 79, 80, 82, 83, 84, 85,
    86
Mallow, Hazel 79
Mallow, Henry 79
Mallow, Herbert 79
Mallow, Jason 79
Mallow, Jasper 79
Mallow, Keith 79
Mallow, Lena (Bennett) 79, 84
Mallow, Michael and Mary
    (Miller) 79
Mallow, Myrtle 79
Mallow, Opal 79
Mallow, Rebecca Jane (Lough)
    79
Mallow, Roy 79
Mallow, Velma 79
Mallow, Warren 79
Maple Grove Lake 1, 78, 83
Maple Grove Lake Restaurant
    86
Maple Grove Lane 28
Maple Hill Cemetery 30
Marion County 34, 37
Marseilles, France 53

Martinsburg, WV 3
Masontown, PA 60
Mauch Chunk formation 67
Mauzy, Hobert and Irene
    (Heitz) 97, 99
Mauzy, Irene (Heitz) 97
Maxwell, Hu 21
Mayle, Reese 42
McBee, Josephine (Harr) 43, 44
McCaffery, Patrick 57
McClain Printing Company
    88, 113
McClellan, General George 22
Meadville, PA 43
Meigs County, OH 94, 95
Meyer Bus Line 28
Meyer, Susan 55
Michigan 15
Middle Ridge Trail 5
Middletown, WV 35
Middle Valley Trail 108
Milkint, Pete 68
Mill Creek, WV 11
Miller, Dave v, 114
Miller, Glenn 59
Mill Run 23, 50
Mingo Indians 35
Mitchell, Grace (Hedrick)
    Hamlin 52
Monongahela National Forest
    71, 104
Monongahela Power 108
Monongahela River 35
Montgomery Ward 40
moonshine 1, 22, 23, 25
Moorefield Junction, WV 10
Morgan, Catherine 35
Morgan, Charles Morgan 34
Morgan, Hannah 34, 35
Morgan, Ivor II 34
Morgan, Morgan 34, 35, 36
Morgan, Nancy 35
Morgan, Susan 34
Morgan, Temperance 35
Morgantown, WV 3, 18, 35, 88,
    92

Index

Morgan, Zackquill 34
Morgan, Zackquill, Bishop of Cardiff 35
Moroney, Mary Jane (Raese) 92
Morrow, William 83
Mosser, Glendie and Naomi 68, 69, 70
Mott, Pearl G. 77
Mt. Storm, WV 75, 80

N

National Fish and Wildlife Foundation 5, 8
Newport News, VA 53, 54
New York 15
New York City 3, 54, 92
Nichols, Chuck v, 114s
Nine, John 18
Northern flying squirrel 93
Northern Methodists 73

O

Oakland, MD 53, 99
Old Timberline Road 5
Onego 79
Osterhout, William 19
Ours, Anna Kate 6
Ours, Bernie Edward 3
Ours, John 3
Ours, Margot (Benthien) 1, 2, 3, 62
Ours, Robert 3
Ours, Sadie (Bell) 2
Ours, Tom 4
Ours, Elliott iii, 2, 3, 7, 8, 62, 88, 89, 90, 91, 110, 114
Ours, Willis 2, 3
Ours, Marguerite (Fleming) 2
outhouse 51
Owens-Illinois Glass Company 48

P

Pacific 54
Pangea 63
Parks, Dana 55

Parsons Advocate 27, 88, 105
Parsons, James 73
Parsons, Virginia (Cooper) 16, 27
Parsons, WV 39, 49, 54, 69, 72
Parsons City Cemetery 27
Patterson, Vernon 25, 26, 93
Paxton, Nancy 35
Pell, Caroline (Miller) 74
Pendleton County 79
Pendleton Run 11, 90
Pentagon 53
Petersburg, WV 28, 29, 37, 42
Phelps, Bill 70
Phelps family 68
Phillips, Cindy 60, 110, 111, 114
Piedmont, WV 72
Pine Ridge 23
Pine Ridge Restaurant 100, 101
Pittman-Robertson Act 104
Pittsburgh, PA 12, 89
planing mill 14
"Platform" 22, 23, 49, 51, 97, 101
Pocono formation 67
Poerschke, Pastor Paul 74, 75, 77
polio 51
Pottsville sandstone 64, 66, 67
Presbyterian 73
Preston County, WV 88
Princeton University 100
Printzler, Eve 33
pulp mill 17

R

Raese brothers 91
Raese, John 81
Raese, Robert and Ann 83
Raese, Walter 92
Rainelle, WV 80
Raines, Carrie 51, 54
Raines, Ethel 54
Raines family 29, 31
Raines, Gabriel and Margaret (Lawrence) 52

Raines, James 51
Raines-Lambert, Rita Anne (Judy) 27, 31
Raines, Lorenzo Dow 51, 54
Rappahannock County, VA 18, 21
Red Creek 51, 52, 67, 79, 96
Red House, MD 52
Reed, Caroline 36
Reed, Randall 101
Refuge Visitor Center 8
Richardson family 68
Ridgway, PA 15
Roberts, Lucille 83
Roberts, Jack 83
Robinson, Felix 73, 77
Roby family 31
Roby, Jeremiah and Charlotte (Griffith) 36
Roby, Lucetta 36, 40
Rodinia 63
Roots in Tucker County 88, 113
rope tow 99, 100
Rowlesburg, WV 18
Route 32 22, 23, 51, 55, 58
Rumbarger 11, 12, 14, 73
Rumbarger, James L. 18

S

Sagace, Joe 101
Sagebrush Lane 37, 58
Saint George, WV 18, 37
Sand Run 5
sandstone 64, 65
saw 14
sawmill 112
Schell, WV 3
Schmelling-Joe Lewis heavyweight title fight 50
Schmitten, Elizabeth 33
school bus 55
Schwarz, Pastor Allen 74, 77
Setterstrom, Jean Ann 55
Shafer, Samuel 39, 46
Shanango, PA 53
Shenandoah County, VA 33

Index

Shenandoah Valley 35
Shepherdstown, WV 4
Shetler, Charles 10
shingle wood factory 14
Shop and Save 53
siltstone 64
Silver Lake 68
Simmons, Connor 95
Sistersville, WV 68
Ski Club of Washington DC 55,
    94, 99, 102, 103
skidders 12, 13
skiing 1, 94
Skinner, Alton 45
Smigal, Alex "Junior" 86
Smigal, Elizabeth "Betty"
    (Mallow) 83, 86
Smigal, Donna, Ann & David
    85, 86
Smith, Albert Norman 43
Smith, Carol 56
Smith, Emily (Warner) 26, 94,
    95, 97, 102, 103
Smith, Hoye and Louise (Heitz)
    29, 81
Smith, Linda 56
Smith, Margaret 43
Smith, Mary Susan 86
snow 50, 99
Social Security 56, 99
Soltow, Pastor Fred 77
Spence, Linnie 26
Spiggle, Wayne C. 29, 83
Spiggle, George Allen 83
splash dam 18, 112, 113
Sprague, Pastor Minor 53
Springer, Drusilla 35
"Springer Place" 80
spruce 14
squatter's rights 22, 23, 24, 25
squirrel 109
Starcher, Larry 24
Stark, Sophia 34, 35
Staron, Veronica (Tekavec) 60,
    108
Stavrakis, Sharon (Parsons) 56, 70

Stewart, Juanita (Pennington)
    31, 78
Steyer, Leon 83
Steyer, Phillip 83
St. John's Lutheran Church iii,
    1, 72, 73, 74, 90
Stony River Dam 13
St. Paul's Lutheran Church 33,
    34
Strasburg, VA 33, 34
Stringtown 58
"Stump Town" 73
Suitland, Maryland 4
Supreme Court of West
    Virginia 17
Swearingen 38
synclines 64

T
Tabor, Judd 43
Taconic Mountains 64, 65
T-bar 100
tectonic plates 62, 63
Tekavec, Frances "Fannie"
    (Zadell) 60
Tekavec, Frank 60
Tennessee 15
Terra Alta, WV 43, 55
Teter, Charles Samuel 113
Teter, Elsie (Cooper) 92
Thanksgiving 27, 109
The Lone Survivor of Camp 72,
    60
Third Street in Davis 72, 73, 90
Thomas Avenue in Davis 73
Thomas, WV 2, 3, 17, 39, 53,
    63, 75, 81
Thompson, Albert 11, 12, 13,
    14, 16, 17, 19
Thompson, Ben 37, 60, 99, 112
Thompson, Dorothy Barbara
    (Mayor) 60
Thompson, Frances 31
Thompson, Frank 11, 20, 55
Thompson, George B. 23, 99,
    112

Thompson Lumber Company
    14, 113
Timberdoodle 8, 111
timber industry 37
Timberline 4, 90, 94
Timberline Resort 107
Timber Ridge 79
Topper, Charlie 3
tourism 77
Tressler Lutheran Associates 76
Tucker County 4, 88, 89
Tucker County Connections
    (TCC) 5
Tucker County Development
    Authority 76
Tucker County Emergency
    Squad 77
Tucker County Highlands
    History and Education
    Project (TCHHEP) i, ii, 8,
    60, 110, 111, 112, 113
Tucker County Historic
    Landmark Commission
    77
Tucker County Hospital 27
Tucker County sheriff 101
Tucker County, WV 10, 18
Twenty Feet from Glory 88

U
Union Drilling Co. 56
University of California
    Museum of Paleontology
    63
Upper Tract 79
US Army 53
US Fish and Wildlife Service ii,
    111
US Geological Survey 88

V
Varsity Restaurant 53
Vietnam 58
Virginia General Assembly 35
Volkswagen Beetle 100

Index

W

Wales 34
Ware, Ruby 58
Warner, Angeline (Nine) 97
Warner, Charles Phillip 97, 98
Warner family 84
Warner, Frank 97, 102
Warner, Hallie 97
Warner, Anna Marie "Mary" or
    "Mountain Ma" (Heitz)
    96, 97, 98, 99, 100, 102,
    103
Washington, DC 4, 52, 58
Watson, Bill 33
Weimer Hollow 69
Weiss Knob 23, 100, 103
Weiss Knob Ski Area 55, 98,
    100, 101, 103
Western Maryland Railroad 13
Western Pocahontas Properties
    107
Westernport, MD 43
West Germany 3
West Penn Power Company 16,
    17
West Virginia and Regional
    History Collection 10
West Virginia Central and
    Pittsburg Railway 18, 20,
    72
West Virginia Conservation
    Commission 104, 105
West Virginia Conservation
    Commission Magazine
    107
West Virginia Department of
    Highways 8
West Virginia Department of
    Natural Resources 57, 104
West Virginia Geological and
    Economic Survey 66
West Virginia House 11
West Virginia Photo Company
    74
West Virginia Pulp and Paper
    Company 19

West Virginia University 3, 10
Wheaton, MD 4
Wheeling, WV 29
White Grass Ski Touring Center
    5, 94
Wiblin family 68
Wild School 8
Williamson, James J. 20
Wilmington, DE 34
Wilmoth family 37
Wilson, George 3, 5
Wilson, Renate (Benthien) 3, 5
Winfred, PA 15
Wolfe family 68
Wolford, Ada 28, 43
Wolford, Amby 28
Wolford, Barton 52
Wolford, Burrell 28
Wolford family 31
Wolford, Feaster 30
Wolford, Floyd and Ida (Raines)
    28
Wolford, Frances (Thompson)
    31
Wolford, Frank 28
Wolford, Jane 41
Wolford, John T. and Narissa
    (Raines) 28
Wolford, Rose 28
Wolford, Ruth 28
Wolford, Sarah Ann (Warner)
    97, 102
Wolford, Tom 28, 29
Wolford, Victor 1, 28, 29, 30
Wonderful West Virginia
    magazine 107
wood hick 41
woodmen 15
Worden, Riley iii, 1, 10, 11
Worden's Hotel 10
World Trade Center 74
World War I 88
World War II 47

Y

Yankee jumper 50
Yeakley, Pastor 75
Young family 68
Young, Simon 95

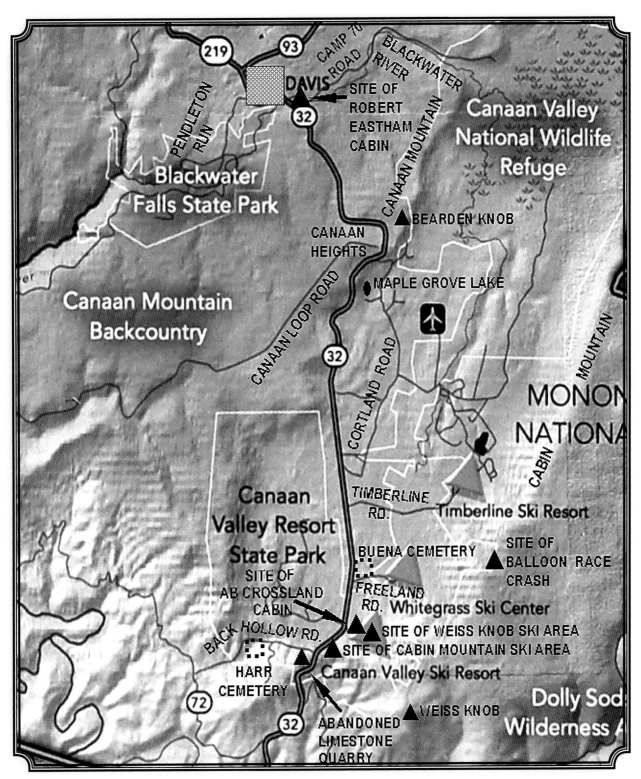

Many of the place names included in this map relate to story locations in
Behold! The Land of Canaan, Volume 2.